Robert Louis Stevenson's

kidnapped

First published in 2003 by Usborne Publishing Ltd,
Usborne House, 83-85 Saffron Hill,
London EC1N 8RT, England.
www.usborne.com

A catalogue record for this title is available
from the British Library.

ISBN 07945 06593

Printed in Great Britain

Series editors: Jane Chisholm and Rosie Dickins
With thanks to Georgina Andrews
Designed by Sarah Cronin
Series designer: Mary Cartwright
Cover design by Stephen Wright and Glen Bird
Cover image © D. Robert & Lorri Franz/CORBIS;
background © Adam Woolfitt/CORBIS

kidnapped

from the story by
Robert Louis Stevenson
retold by Henry Brook

Illustrated by Bob Harvey

Contents

About *Kidnapped*

First published in 1886, *Kidnapped* is now acknowledged as one of Robert Louis Stevenson's greatest novels. It describes sixteen-year-old David Balfour's struggle to outwit his evil uncle, Ebenezer, and claim his rightful inheritance. ("Balfour" was Stevenson's mother's maiden name and one of his own middle names.) Stevenson always claimed that he believed the purpose of writing books was "to entertain and not to educate", and in the original dedication to his novel he modestly declared that his only intention was to "steal a young gentleman's attention" from his school books. But *Kidnapped* is much more than a thrilling adventure story. It gives the reader a portrait of war-torn Scotland in the year 1751, and provides a rich description of how the Highland clans (or tribes) lived at the time.

Stevenson was born in Edinburgh in 1850 and was always fascinated by the history of his country. He was proud to be a Scot, but his health was too weak to endure the harsh Scottish weather. As a child he was often confined to bed, and as a young university student there were days when his chest was so sensitive, it caused him agony to wear even a light cotton jacket. Doctors told him that if he wanted to live for more than a few more years he must migrate to a warm and dry climate. This enforced absence made the author feel like an exile from his own country. *Kidnapped* was written while he lived in a small resort town in the south of England, where he was terribly homesick. He wrote *The Strange Case of Dr. Jekyll and Mr. Hyde* in the same year, and although that book is supposed to be set in London, most of the character's names are Scottish and the urban descriptions have more in common with Edinburgh than they do with the English capital. In *Kidnapped*, Stevenson no longer had to disguise his wish to write about the Scottish countryside he longed to revisit. In all his stories, he liked to include lots of old Scottish words, some of which are no longer used. This version of *Kidnapped* has been updated to modern English.

The book was inspired by the real–life assassination of Colin Campbell – an agent for the English king – in 1752, and the subsequent trial of James Stewart for the murder. Stevenson was interested in the background tensions that led up to the killing and trial and he crafted his story using some of the known facts. The book that resulted is a gripping story with a breathless pace, and it features two of Stevenson's greatest characters – David Balfour and Alan Breck.

These two meet each other at a time when Scotland was divided by religion. In the northern part of the country, the Highlands, the clans were mainly Catholic. But in the south, the Lowlands, the people were Protestants. The last great uprising of the clans took place in 1745, and in 1746 they were finally defeated by English forces at the battle of Culloden. Although *Kidnapped* uses these events in part for its framework, Stevenson was looking further back in history to provide the atmosphere for his novel – to the time of the Celts, the first settlers in the Highlands, who arrived before Roman times. He wanted to explore the great variety of influences that had contributed to the Scottish national character.

At one point, David Balfour finds himself shipwrecked on the west coast of Scotland. But Stevenson suggests that his Lowland hero could have been dropped into a foreign country. David feels like an alien in his own land. The people he encounters speak a language he can't understand (Gaelic), their customs are unfamiliar and the way they organize their society is different from his own. Some of the traditions of the Highland clans were inherited from the Celts: music, language and dress for instance. Stevenson forces David to confront this Celtic influence by introducing the highlander, Alan Breck. Alan rescues David from a bloodthirsty ship's crew and guides him to safety across the wild Highland landscape. He speaks Gaelic and lives by the sword, like a warrior from an earlier age.

The conflict between David and Alan – two Scots who seem to inhabit different countries – is one of the things that makes *Kidnapped* such a great story. Although he states that he wrote to entertain, throughout his life Stevenson tried to understand the customs and beliefs of the other world cultures he visited (see *About Robert Louis Stevenson* at the end of this book). Through the character of Alan Breck he describes the "warrior traditions" of the Highland clans, and the clash with David's Lowland values. But, despite all their disagreements, the two Scotsmen unite against the dangers they face and become close friends. Their shared belief in the values of honesty and loyalty as they battle the rogues and pirates they come across in the story, binds them together like blood brothers.

The Letter of Inheritance

If anyone tells you life is a dull and predictable business, let them hear my story. In the year 1751 I lost my parents and my home. I was sixteen years old and all I possessed were the clothes on my back. I had nowhere to go, and no reason to think my life would amount to much. But over the following weeks I had more adventures than most people see in a lifetime. I learned how it feels to be rich, and what it means to be a slave. I saw sword fights and shipwrecks and was an outlaw in my own country. But I'll begin at the beginning, in a sleepy village in Scotland…

It was a fine, summer morning as I locked the door of my father's house for the last time. The blackbirds were whistling among the garden flowers, and the dawn mist had started to lift and die away. The church minister, Mr. Campbell, was waiting for me at the gate.

"Have you had any breakfast, Davie?" he asked kindly.

I nodded my head.

"Well, I will go with you as far as the ford crossing, to see you on your way."

After a few minutes of walking together in silence, Mr. Campbell turned to me. "Are you sorry to leave the village of Essendean?"

"Well, sir," I replied, "I've been very happy here, but now that my parents are both dead, I'll be no nearer to them in Essendean than I would if I was on the other side of the world, or any other place. There are good memories here, and some sad ones. So, if I knew where I could find work and build a life for myself, I would go there gladly."

The minister smiled and gave me a pat on my shoulder. "I have something to tell you, Davie, something that will change your life forever."

He looked around for somewhere to sit and, spying a flat-topped boulder by the side of the road, led me over to it. The sun was beating down on us now, and I could smell the scent of the wild flowers and the heather, drifting down from the open country at the top of the valley. I sat next to him on the rock and he took my hand.

"When your mother was dead," he began in a serious voice, "and your father himself was dying, he gave me a letter, which he said was your inheritance. 'Once I am gone,' he told me, 'and the house has been emptied, give my boy this letter and send him off to the House of Shaws, in the district of Cramond. That is where I am from, and it seems right that my son should return there.' That was his request, Davie.

"I always had my suspicions that your father was well-born. His manners and conversation were not those of a common schoolteacher. The House of Shaws is an ancient, honest and respected family name, though these days the estate is somewhat decayed."

"Estate?" I stammered in my excitement. The minister slowly reached inside his cloak and took out an envelope. It was addressed:

To be delivered to Ebenezer Balfour,
of The House of Shaws,
by my son, David Balfour.

"Congratulations, Davie," he laughed. "You should reach Cramond, which is near Edinburgh, in two days. If the worst happens, and your rich relations turn you away, then come straight back to my door. But I'm sure they'll invite you to stay, as your father believed."

Then, with an uplifted, waggling finger, and a stern voice to accompany it, he warned me about the variety of evils I might encounter in the world. Next, he said a few words about how I should behave with my new relatives. "Remember, you have been brought up in the country. Don't shame us with any 'farm boy' bad manners. In that great house, with all its servants, try not to say anything stupid. As for the laird – don't forget he is master of the estate. It's a pleasure for a Scotsman to obey a good laird."

"I promise to do my best, sir."

He hugged me, then held me at arm's length, studying me with a sad expression. At last he cried "goodbye" and set off back to the village at a run. It was a strange sight to watch the minister jogging away from me, but I realized he was unhappy to see me go, and had to get away before his emotions got the better of him.

I knew I should feel sad too, but I was longing to meet my new family. After scolding myself for such ungrateful thoughts, when I was saying farewell to my only friend, I waded the ford and climbed the side of the valley. Out on the drover's road that runs wide through the heather, I turned and took my last look at the church of Essendean, the tall, wind-curled trees around its graveyard and the rowan trees with their bright red berries, marking the spot where my mother and father rested. Then I was on my way.

Two days later I spotted Edinburgh, with thousands of chimneys smoking like a forest fire, high upon a ridge that ran down to the sea. There was a flag on the highest castle tower and a flotilla of ships bobbing around by the docks. I starcd at this scene for hours, my country eyes amazed by the new sights of the ocean and the city.

Coming down onto the road for Cramond, I saw a regiment of English soldiers, marching in perfect step to a tune played on the Highland pipes. At the head of the column was an old, red-faced general, who rode a grey horse. The gold buttons on their red uniforms glittered in the sun, and the pipe music made me want to start marching myself.

I asked the people I met for directions to "The House of Shaws". But the question surpriscd everyone. At first I thought it must be that my dusty, travel-worn appearance was so unlike the grand tradition of that name, but I soon began to wonder if there might be something strange about the Shaws themselves.

I decided to pose my qucstions more carefully. Seeing a man driving down the lane in a cart, I asked him if he had heard of the house.

"I have," he answered. "Why do you want to know?"

"Is it a large place?" I continued.

"It's a big house, that's for sure."

"But what about the people that live in it?" I tried.

"People?" he shouted. "What people?"

"But, there's Mr. Ebenezer," I said, my voice wobbling a little.

"Oh, the laird," the man growled. "What's your business with *him*?"

"I was told I might be able to get a job there," I lied, still hoping for more information.

"A job?" he screamed, so loudly his horse almost bolted. "Listen, boy, you look like a good lad to me. If you'll take a word of advice, you'll stay away from the House of Shaws, *and* its laird."

If it hadn't been two days walk back to the cozy fireside of Mr. Campbell, I might have turned around, then and there. But I knew I had to go on and discover the truth for myself, and deliver my father's letter.

Towards sundown I saw a woman in a ragged, black cloak, trudging down a slope. Despite the sour expression on her face, I asked her if she knew the House of Shaws. Silently, she led me to the summit of the hill she had just descended.

"There," she hissed.

The next valley was a collection of pretty fields and low hills, specked with streams and clumps of woods. In the middle of the plain was a huge house, that looked a bit more like a ruin than a place of residence. There was no road running up to it, no smoke from the chimneys, and no garden that I could see.

"That is the place," she spat at me. She was trembling with a sudden anger. "Blood built it," she cried, "blood stopped the building of it, and blood shall bring it down." She waved her fist in the air. "I curse the laird and his estate. I curse his house, his stable, and every man, woman and child that goes near the place." She turned and was off on her way.

I stood there, shocked, my hair standing on end. In those days, people still believed in witches, and after hearing her terrible curse I was shaking so much my teeth chattered. I rested on the hill, not sure if I should retreat or advance.

At last, I saw a tiny line of smoke curling from one of the chimneys. It was hardly more than a puff, but it proved there was some life in that old pile of stones. So, I went down the hill along a faint track that meandered toward the house.

It was truly a beautiful valley; streaked with hawthorn bushes full of flowers, sheep roaming in the fields and a flurry of birds in the sky. But the closer I got to the wreck of the house, the drearier it seemed. Where the upper stories should have been, I could see open staircases and piles of stones that showed the builders had left before completing their work. Most of the windows had no glass in them, and bats flew in and out of the rooms like bees around a hive.

I stepped forward cautiously and, over the murmur of the wind, I heard the clatter of dishes and a dry, rasping cough. But there was no sound of voices – not even the bark of a dog.

The main door was tall and studded with old rusty nails. I knocked once, and the house fell into dead silence. A whole minute passed and nothing stirred except the bats fluttering around my head. Again I knocked. By now, my ears were so used to the quiet, I could hear the faint tick of a clock, deep inside the house. But whoever had been coughing now kept completely still and must have held his breath.

I was in two minds about whether to knock again or give up, but my anger got the better of me. I started raining kicks and punches on the door, shouting out for Mr. Balfour to show himself.

Suddenly I heard the cough directly above me and I jumped back from the door. I could see a man in a nightcap, and the black muzzle of a huge gun pointing straight at me.

"It's loaded," said a thin, creaking voice.

"I have a letter," I answered boldly. "For Mr. Ebenezer Balfour. Is he here?"

"Put it down on the doorstep and clear off," said the man, crouching behind his gun.

"I will do no such thing," I shouted, my anger making me brave. "It is a letter of introduction and it must be passed into Mr. Balfour's hands."

"Introducing who?" the voice asked.

"I am not ashamed of my name," I replied. "I am David Balfour."

I heard the gun barrel rattling on the windowsill, and thought I saw the nightcap bob up and down, as though the man was so shocked he was shaking violently.

"Is your father dead?" he managed to say.

I was too surprised by the question to give an answer.

"I see," he resumed, in a crafty voice. "He must be dead. That'll be what brings you beating on my door. Well, Master Balfour," he said after a long pause, "I'll let you in." And he disappeared from the window.

There was a loud rattling of chains and bolts, and the door was slowly opened and shut behind me as soon as I had passed through.

"Go into the kitchen and don't touch anything," ordered the voice from the shadows. I groped my way into a large room.

The firelight showed me the barest habitation I had ever lain eyes on. There were some dishes on a shelf and a table set with a bowl of porridge and a small cup of beer. That was all there was in that huge, stone-walled room, except for a few padlocked chests.

As soon as he had fastened his chains around the door, the man came through to join me. He was a mean-looking, stooping, wax-faced creature, aged somewhere between fifty and seventy. He wore a rough nightgown over a crumpled shirt. I couldn't guess when he had last shaved, and his fingernails were long and yellow as corn. But what distressed me more than his appearance was the way he stared. He couldn't take his eyes off me, but didn't dare look me straight in the face. I guessed he was an old servant who had been left in charge of the house while its owner was away.

"If you're hungry," he snarled, "you can eat a bit of my porridge."

"I wouldn't want to steal your dinner."

"I don't need it," he answered. "Though I'll keep the beer. It helps my cough."

He took a swig from the cup and then put his hand out. "Let's see the letter."

"But it's for Mr. Balfour," I answered defiantly. "And for his eyes only."

"And who do you think I am?" he shrieked. "Give me Alexander's letter."

"You know my father's name?" I gasped.

"It would be strange if I didn't," he said, smirking. "He was my brother, and little as you seem to like me, my house *or* my porridge, I'm your uncle, Ebenezer."

I was so disappointed by this news that I almost burst into tears. But I controlled myself, handed him the envelope and sat down to poke at the bowl of cold porridge in disgust. My uncle went over to the fireplace and examined his letter carefully.

"Do you know what's in it?" he asked, when he had finished his inspection.

"There's a wax seal on it, isn't there?" I asked, annoyed that he thought I might have opened a private note.

"So, what made you come here?"

"To give you my father's letter."

"No, I mean, what other hopes did you have?" he asked slyly.

"I confess, sir," I answered, "I did get excited when I heard I was linked to a good family name. And I did think I might get some help with a start in life. But I am no beggar. I might look poor, but I have other friends who will be pleased to help me, if I was mistaken."

"Calm yourself," muttered Ebenezer. "Don't lose your temper so quickly, boy. We'll get along fine.

Now, if you're finished with my porridge, I might have a taste of it myself."

Before I could answer he had pushed me from my seat and was digging into his supper. "Your father loved meat," he said, still chomping. "Oh, he was a hearty eater, but I never cared much for my food." He slurped on the beer and, glancing up at me, added, "If you're thirsty, you'll find a bucket of water by the door."

I watched him spooning the porridge between his thin, pale lips and realized he was still scrutinizing me. Our gaze met only once, when he thought I was staring into the fire and I turned suddenly. No thief caught with his hand in a man's pocket could have looked as guilty. But there was something else I discerned, from studying his expression. He was scared of me.

"Has your father been dead a long time?" he asked suddenly.

"Three weeks, sir."

"He was a secretive type," Ebenezer mumbled, half to himself. "He never said much when he was young. He never spoke of me, did he?"

"I didn't know he had a brother until you told me."

"Dear me," he said. "And nothing about the Shaws either?"

"Nothing, sir."

Uncle Ebenezer seemed more cheerful after we'd had this conversation. I couldn't be sure if he was upset to hear of his brother's death or if it had been the arrival of a stranger that had troubled him, but perhaps I had judged him too quickly. He came up behind me and gave me a slap across the back.

"We'll be friends before you know it," he laughed. "And now I'll show you to your bed."

To my surprise, he didn't light a candle or a lamp, but started off into a dim passage that led away from the kitchen, feeling his way up a flight of steps. It was so pitch-dark I couldn't see where I was putting my feet. I stumbled after him and when we reached the landing he guided me into a room.

"Uncle, could I have a light please?"

"You don't need one," he snapped. "There's a bright moon tonight."

"There's no moon or any stars in the sky," I protested, "and it's so dark in here I can't even see the bed."

I could hear him sneering behind me. "I don't like too many lights in my house. They're a fire risk. Good night, nephew."

And before I could answer he had closed the door and locked me in. I stood there in the blackness, not sure if I should laugh or cry. The room was as cold as the bottom of a well, and the bed (when I managed to find it), nearly as damp. By good luck, I'd brought my things up with me from the kitchen, and the cloth I'd used to make my travel bundle served as well to make a snug bundle of me.

And then, despite all the strange events of the past two days, I fell into a heavy and dreamless sleep.

In the Dark Tower

I woke early in brilliant sunlight. It took ten minutes of shouting and hammering on the door before I heard my uncle shuffling around in the hallway. After releasing me and grunting "good morning", he led me down to the kitchen where he'd set breakfast across the table. There were two bowls of porridge but only one small cup of beer. He must have noticed that I was staring at the single drink because he asked me if I'd like some myself.

"I would, but not if it's any trouble for you."

"No trouble at all," he replied.

Then, to my considerable amazement, I watched as he fetched another tiny cup and carefully poured half the beer from his cup into the new one. This sharing would have been noble if my uncle had been a very poor man and was giving me half of all that he had. But I knew he must have money, because all the farmers on his estate would pay him rent. So he must be a miser, and a very miserly one at that.

After breakfast he asked me questions about my time in Essendean. "Is your mother dead too?"

I nodded my head.

"She was a pretty girl," he sighed. "I'm proud of

our family name, Davie," he spoke up in a confident voice, "and I'll do what's right by you. But it's going to take me a while to decide which career is most suitable for you: the church, the law, or the army. In the meantime, I don't want any visitors disturbing us."

"What are you getting at, uncle?" I asked him, feeling a little uneasy at the way the conversation was going.

"I don't want you to send any letters or messages to your friends."

"If I want to write to a friend, I will," I said angrily. "I don't need your permission to do anything."

"Don't lose your temper again, boy," he said softly. "You belong here, in the House of Shaws, and I want to help you."

"It seems a strange way to go about it," I answered.

"All I ask is that you give me a few days, without interruptions, to make my arrangements. In a day or two, you'll get what you deserve."

"Very well," I said, reluctantly. "I know I should be grateful for your help. You have my word I won't bring any new visitors to your door."

"Blood's thicker than water, Davie," he whispered with a wolfish smile. "You let the two of us Balfours work things out in peace."

For a day that began so badly, I have to say I enjoyed the rest of it. We had more porridge for lunch – this was the extent of my uncle's diet – and in the afternoon I explored the house library. There were both English and Latin volumes there and I spent most of the day in the good company of literature.

But I made a curious discovery. As I opened the cover of one of the books, I saw some faint handwriting and immediately recognized it as my father's.

To my brother Ebenezer, on his fifth birthday

This made no sense to me. Knowing that my father must be the younger brother - because otherwise it would have been he who had inherited the house and not Ebenezer - either he had made some mistake with the birthday, or he had mastered writing at a very early age.

I tried to get the puzzle out of my head but, whatever I did, I couldn't stop thinking about it. So, when I went back into the kitchen and sat down for our dinner - cold porridge, of course - I decided to question my uncle.

"Did my father learn reading and writing at a younger age than most children?" I asked him.

"Alexander?" he scoffed, between spoonfuls. "I was much quicker. I could read as soon as he could."

"I don't understand," I muttered, more puzzled than ever. "Were you and my father twins?"

Ebenezer coughed and the spoon shot out of his mouth. One of his bony hands scrabbled at my collar.

"Why are you asking about that?" he demanded. His mouth was twitching and his eyes were sparkling like glass beads.

"Take your hand off my jacket." I said calmly, knowing full well that I was twice as strong as he was. He let go and slumped across the table, reaching for his spoon.

"He was my only brother, Davie," he spluttered. "You shouldn't speak to me about him. It upsets me too much."

As I watched him, shaking in his chair, I remembered the words of an old folk song, about a poor beggar boy who was the rightful heir to a great fortune, and a wicked relative who tried to cheat him out of it. In Scottish law, at this time in history, the title and property of a man passed down to his oldest son, and not to any of the other siblings.

The more I thought of it, the more suspicious I became of my uncle. We sat at the table, ignoring our porridge and staring at each other the way a cat stares at a mouse.

"Davie," he began suddenly, "I've just remembered something. Before you were born, I told your father I'd put a little money aside for you. It wasn't a legal contract, of course, just a gentleman's promise. I've always kept that money for you and it has now grown to be, precisely..." he hesitated, and I could see him frantically trying to find the words, "precisely, twenty pounds."

I guessed the whole story was a lie, even though I didn't understand his motives. "Come now, uncle," I whispered, not disguising my mockery of him, "think again. Surely you mean, thirty pounds."

"That's what I said," he screeched. "And if you'll step outside for a moment, I'll fetch it for you."

I did as he asked, smiling to myself that he thought I could be so easily deceived. If it was true that my father was the older brother, then the estate should have been his and I would inherit everything. Uncle Ebenezer wouldn't be able to claim as much as his porridge spoon.

But I couldn't be sure this was the case, so I waited patiently for my uncle to call me back into the kitchen. The night was warm but there was a wind moaning up in the valley hills. It sounded like a distant sea, pounding against a shore. The air was heavy and had the scent of sparks on a stone, as though there was a storm threatening.

Ebenezer called me in and counted a pile of gold coins into my hand. When he reached twenty-seven, his miserly heart couldn't stand it any more, and he shoved the rest of the change into his pocket.

"To cover my expenses," he sighed. "But don't say I don't keep my word. I'll always do my best for my brother's son."

I thanked him, watching him carefully for any tricks. And then I felt like an ungrateful wretch. It was possible that I was wrong about my father, and Ebenezer was the proper heir. I felt guilty for suspecting him.

"And one good turn deserves another," he whispered.

"I am ready to prove my thanks," I answered.

"I'm getting old," he replied. "Some help with the house and garden chores would be appreciated."

"Of course, uncle," I replied. "I'd be happy to help you."

"Let's get started then," he said, clapping his hands together. He pulled a huge, rusty key from his shirt pocket. "This opens the door to the tower, at the end of the house. But you'll have to go outside to reach it. There's an old chest right at the top. Bring it to me. I need some papers from it, that concern my plans for your future."

"Can I have a light, sir?"

"Sorry, Davie," he said, scowling at me. "You know I don't like lights."

"Are the stairs safe?" I asked him.

"They're solid, don't worry. There's no central banister so keep to the wall. But the stairs are as good as new, I promise."

I told him I'd be back in a few minutes, and stepped out into the night.

The wind was still booming in the hills but it was all calm around the house. There were no stars, and it was so dark I had to feel my way along the wall. I'd reached the tower and was fiddling with the key in the lock when the whole sky flashed with fire and went black again. The brightness of this summer lightning made my eyes water and I was blinking as I pushed my way into the tower. I waited for the accompanying boom of thunder but all was quiet, so I decided the lightning was a solitary wanderer from some distant storm.

Inside the tower it was so dark I had to reach out with a hand to find the bottom of the stair case. I found a ledge of stone and realized it must be the first step. It was smooth and solid, just as my uncle had said. Keeping close to the wall I lifted my foot and found the next stair, and then I was off, climbing into the blackness.

The House of Shaws was five floors high, and I knew it would take me a while to reach the top. As I advanced, I thought I detected a change in the temperature of the air and the depth of the darkness in the stairwell. I paused, waiting to see if my eyes could make out anything strange, when a second flash of lightning ripped across the sky above me.

I would have screamed at what I saw, but the cold grip of fear was choking my throat. The lightning shone in on me from every side, through huge gaps and jagged tears in the brickwork. It was as though I was standing inside a tower made of scaffolding poles, and not sturdy walls. But this horror was nothing compared to what I'd seen at my feet. The staircase was built with stone slabs for steps. These slabs were fixed into holes in the tower wall. But they all extended by different lengths. I was standing on a short step. One inch to the right, of my right foot, the step vanished and I was staring into the black pit below.

So these were the "solid" steps my uncle had promised me. He had sent me up here hoping I would be too scared to complete the task he'd set me. The thought of him cackling away in the kitchen filled me with fury. In my pride, I swore to myself that I'd finish the job and throw the chest down at his feet.

I got down on my hands and knees and started to climb, like a mountaineer, testing each new step before I moved from the one I was already on. The darkness grew even blacker and I was alarmed to hear

a whistling and crackling coming from above me. It was a swarm of bats, crashing down inside the tower, beating around my ears and face as they flew past. But still I climbed steadily upwards.

At a turn in the staircase, I put my left hand out and my whole body began tilting forward. There was nothing but empty space before me. I pulled myself back and carefully examined the edge of the last step. The staircase I was on came to a dead stop, hanging in empty space, one hundred feet above the ground.

My uncle wasn't trying to scare me, as I had thought. He had murder on his mind. The staircase had never been finished. If I hadn't been testing each step, I would have stepped out into the void that now gaped before me.

I groped my way back down the stairs and crept back to the kitchen. Ebenezer was at the table with his back to me, glugging from a bottle of whisky. His body shuddered and he was groaning loudly, perhaps struggling with pangs of guilt at plotting my murder. I tiptoed up to him and grabbed him by the shoulder.

My uncle bleated like a sheep and fell to the floor like a dead man. A drenching from a bucket of ice-cold water soon brought him back to life.

"Are you a ghost?" he spluttered, his eyes full of terror.

"Not yet, uncle. Though it's no thanks to you."

His breathing was loud and gasping, and he suddenly clamped a hand to his heart. "Get me the blue bottle, in the cupboard. Please, Davie."

I found the medicine and gave him a sip, then propped him up in a chair.

"My heart is weak," he whispered. "Take me to my bed."

I felt a little sorry for him, but the memory of the tower was still fresh in my mind. "I've a few questions to ask you first."

He shook his head. "I'll answer everything in the morning. I promise."

"I know about your promises."

"Please, Davie," he begged me. He was so weak I couldn't refuse him. I followed him up to his room and locked him in, just as he had imprisoned me the previous night. Downstairs, I threw more coal on the fire than it had seen for years in that miser's kitchen, and stretched out in front of the blaze, ready for sleep.

In the morning I washed my face and replenished the fire, then sat pondering my future. There was no doubt that my uncle had wanted to kill me and I should face up to the fact that there was every chance he would try again. But, like many a lad who was country-bred, I had a high opinion of my own cleverness and cunning. Gazing into the roaring coals, I was confident that I could win any battle of wits between us.

After an hour had passed, I went upstairs and released him. He said "good morning," politely, and soon we were scoffing our breakfast porridge, as though nothing had happened.

"Well, sir," I said, with a jeering tone, "have you anything to say to me?"

He stared into his breakfast bowl in silence.

"You took me for a country fool, and I took you for an honest man. It seems we were both mistaken. Tell me why you fear me, cheat me and make an attempt on my life."

He muttered that he would explain everything after breakfast, and I could see that he was buying time, in order to concoct some lie. Just as I was about to tell him this, there was a knock at the front door.

I opened it to see a young boy dressed in sailor's clothes. As soon as he saw me he started dancing, at what I could only imagine was a sailor's jig, snapping his fingers and carefully positioning his feet. Despite his happy dance, I could see he was trembling with the cold and there was something in his face, an expression somewhere between tears and laughter that made him look desperately sad.

"Morning to you, mate," he sang out in a peculiar accent.

"What's your business?" I asked.

"I've a letter from old 'easy-oasy, for 'Mr. Bellflower'. And I'm almost dead with hunger."

I smiled and asked him in for some of our breakfast. He set about the porridge as though he hadn't eaten for weeks, all the time making silly faces and winking at me, perhaps thinking it would make me like him. It had the opposite effect. My uncle studied the letter and then called me over to a corner of the room. "Read it," he whispered.

The Hawes Inn at the Queen's Ferry

SIR - I'm docked here and about to sail, as the wind is up this afternoon. If you have any further commands for overseas business you must come today.

Your humble servant -
Elias Hoseason

"You see, Davie," my uncle began in an excited voice, "I have some business with this man Hoseason, the captain of a trading ship, the *Covenant*. If we walk over to Queensferry with this cabin boy he's sent, I could see the captain and then visit my lawyer, Mr. Rankeillor. You don't trust me and I don't blame you, but you'll trust Rankeillor. He represents all the gentry in these parts and is a highly respected character. And he knew your father."

I studied my uncle and thought about his plan. Anywhere that had a dock and quayside must have lots of people around and so it would be unlikely he would try to harm me. The company of the cabin boy also offered me some protection. Then there was the lawyer, who sounded as though he might know the truth about my inheritance. And, lastly, I have to admit that I was longing to take a closer look at one of the sailing ships I'd heard so much about, and only glimpsed for the first time three days ago, on the outskirts of Edinburgh.

"Very well," I said decisively, "let's go to the ferry."

It was June and the grass was white with the petals of daisies and the trees with blossom. But after walking a mile we were so cold it might as well have been winter, and the whiteness a December frost. I chatted with the cabin boy who said his name was Ransome.

He said he'd been at sea since he was nine, but wasn't sure how old he was because he'd lost track of the years. His chest was covered in blurred tattoos, he swore horribly (but more like an idiot schoolboy than a man), and he boasted of all the terrible things he'd done, few of which I believed possible. When I asked him about Captain Hoseason, he told me he was a rough, ruthless and brutal man. But Ransome thought these were good qualities in a sailor.

"His only flaw," he stuttered in the biting wind, "is his seamanship. He relies on Mr. Shaun, the navigator, in that department. Mr. Shaun is a fine man, except for his drinking. It makes him lash out."

He pulled up a leg of his trousers and showed me a deep, raw wound in his calf that made my blood run cold.

"But you're not a slave," I protested. "You can't let an officer do that to you."

"I won't let it happen again," answered Ransome, with a smirk. And he pulled a long knife from his jacket.

I felt sorry for Ransome, a foolish boy trapped on board a hell upon the seas, with cruel and violent masters.

We crested the rim of a line of hills and below us was the ferry and the Firth of Forth, the wide estuary that opens out onto the sea. On the western side it narrows into the width of a river and I could see the line of a pier where the ferry must sail from, and standing next to it, in a pretty garden of holly trees and hawthorns, the "Hawes Inn".

The town of Queensferry was a mile or two further to the west and, as the ferry had just left for the north bank, there weren't many people around. There was a small boat pulled up on the shore and a few sailors lounging around. Ransome informed me that this was the captain's boat, and it was called a "skiff". Half a mile out in the firth was the *Covenant* herself, her decks bustling with all the preparation for her voyage. After what Ransome had told me, I feared for all those who were condemned to sail in that sinister hulk of a ship.

At the inn, Ransome led us up a winding stairway to a gloomy room in the loft. It was as hot as an oven, heated by a blazing coal fire. The captain, a bulky, solemn-looking man, was sitting at a small table. Despite the heat, he wore a thick jacket buttoned to the neck, and a hat pulled down over his ears. He came over and shook Ebenezer's hand.

"I am glad you're here in time," he boomed in a deep voice. "The tide turns in an hour and we'll be riding along with it."

I was feeling faint with the stifling heat in that room and my uncle was already mopping his brow with his handkerchief.

"I take it you feel the cold, captain?" asked Ebenezer, with a weak smile.

"I've ice in my heart instead of blood," answered the captain. "I've spent too many years roasting in the tropic seas, to break into a sweat in Scotland."

My uncle dragged a chair across to the table. I wondered if the old miser enjoyed a bit of free heating. But, as for me, the stuffy atmosphere in the room was turning my stomach. Even though I'd promised myself I wouldn't let my uncle out of sight for a moment, when the captain suggested I get some fresh air outside I hastily agreed.

I wandered out along the beach, sniffing the unfamiliar salt air. The sailors around the skiff were spread out on the sand, enjoying a last touch of the solid ground before the months they would spend at sea. They were big men, burned by the sun. One of them had a pair of pistol handles poking from his jacket, and the others had knives or vicious-looking bludgeons sticking out of their pockets.

The sea air had given me an appetite and I walked back to the inn. When the landlord came over with a plate of food for me, I decided to test my uncle's story.

"Have you heard of a Mr. Rankeillor, sir?" I asked.

"Of course I have," he answered jovially. "He's the most honest man in the district."

"That's what I was hoping," I replied.

"Did you come in with Ebenezer?" he asked, and I could see he was studying me carefully.

"I did."

"Are you related by any chance?"

I thought this over for a second. I had a feeling the landlord was about to tell me something important about my uncle and I didn't want to put him off by letting him know I was of the same family. "Oh, no," I told him, feeling a little guilty about the lie.

"Your face reminds me of his brother, Alexander."

"I wouldn't know about that," I said. "Was he as unpopular as Ebenezer seems to be?"

"No, he was as good as Ebenezer is wicked," the landlord said with a sigh. "I know people who'd like to see Ebenezer with a noose around his neck. But he was a fine man once. That was before the whisper went round that he'd killed his brother."

"But why would he do that?"

"To get the house, lad. Alexander was the elder son. But one summer he disappeared, and Ebenezer turned into a black-hearted miser. Enjoy your lunch."

He left me at the table, stunned by my good fortune. Of course I'd had my suspicions, but now they'd been confirmed. The whole estate, the ancient house, the surrounding valley of fields and cottages, it all belonged to me. I gazed out of the inn window, trying to imagine myself as "a laird".

After a few minutes I saw the skiff being pulled down from the beach into the water. The captain was marching over from the inn, his face grave and serious. He spoke with the gathered sailors for a moment and I was impressed with his gentlemanly poise and bearing, compared with the other seafarers with their torn clothes and savage faces. I wondered if Ransome's stories could be true. The captain struck me as a noble and honest man, not the merciless brute that had been described.

I heard my uncle's reedy voice calling for me, and saw him join the captain on the beach. Leaving a coin for the landlord, I hurried out to meet them.

"Mr. David Balfour, sir," the captain said, "your uncle has told me great things about you. I only wish we had a little more time to become firm friends."

I was flattered by his words and there was a blush on my cheek. A sea captain had called me "sir". Already I was thinking of my new position as a laird, and my standing in society.

"Would you join me in my cabin?" the captain asked warmly. "We could enjoy a glass of wine before I sail."

For a second I hesitated. I longed to see the inside of an ocean-going ship, especially on a private tour of the captain's quarters, but I knew I had to be careful until I'd had a chance to speak to the lawyer, Mr. Rankeillor, about my rightful inheritance.

"It's very kind of you, captain," I replied, "but my uncle and I have an appointment to keep."

"Yes, with your family lawyer," he said with a smile. "Ebenezer has mentioned it. Don't worry about that, I'll send you back in the skiff in good time for the meeting."

And then, seeing that Ebenezer was staring out

toward the ocean, he suddenly leaned close to my ear.

"You must be wary of the old fox, your uncle," he whispered. "I know about his plans. Come aboard and while I show you around, we can talk in private."

I realized I had to trust the captain, who seemed to be looking out for my best interests, so I let him take me by the arm and lead me over to the skiff. In a few minutes of rowing against the waves we were bobbing by the side of the ship. I stared up at the mighty masts, and listened to the creaks and groans of the huge deck timbers as the *Covenant* swayed on the tide. One of the sailors dropped a rope with a loop tied into it over the side and Hoseason was winched aboard. I was next and as soon as I landed on the boards he took me by the arm and guided me into the middle of the deck. I stood there a moment, feeling dizzy with the dip and roll of the vessel, while the captain pointed out the different parts of the rigging and told me the names of the sailors.

"But where is my uncle?" I asked, suddenly.

A grim smile spread across the captain's lips as he hissed at me, "He's not coming with us on this trip, Davie."

With all my strength I tore myself free from his grip and ran over to the ship's side. There was the skiff, moving quickly back to town, with my uncle crouched at the stern.

"Uncle, please help me," I screamed across the waves. He turned around in his seat and even though he was some way off, I could see a cruel and sneering expression of triumph on his face.

That was the last thing I saw. I was dragged from the side of the ship, and then a thunderbolt seemed to strike me on the back of my head. There was a great flash of fire, and then nothing but the darkness.

Galley Slave

When I came to, my head was pounding with noise outside and pain inside, my hands and feet were tied with a chaffing rope and I was still in darkness. For a moment I feared that I might be blind, but then I saw a crack of light above me, and slowly realized where I must be.

I was locked in the belly of the ship, and judging by the violent pitch and roll of the timbers, we were out in the deep water, fighting a storm. With a howl of pain I remembered my stupidity in trusting the captain. The thought of everything I had lost, and the expression of victory on my uncle's face as he made his way back to shore, was enough to make me weep.

It was impossible to tell how much time passed in that dripping, rat-infested cell beneath the waves, but at last I heard a voice above me and felt a gust of fresh air brush my face.

"He has a fever, sir," said a kind voice. "Look for yourself."

I heard a grunt behind him and guessed it was the captain.

"He looks fine to me, Mr. Riach."

"No sir," the first voice pleaded. "He must be

taken out of here at once."

"Not till we sight the American coast. Now I must get back to the deck."

I managed to lift my head but I was too weak to say anything. The captain was climbing a rope ladder up to the open hatch but the other man caught him by his jacket sleeve.

"I did not take you for a murderer, sir," he cried.

The captain shook the hand off his cuff and his eyes flickered in rage. "You'll watch your tongue with me, Mr. Riach." But he paused on the ladder and, looking over his shoulder at me, he added, "Will he die?"

The other man nodded his head grimly.

"Bring him up then," spat the captain, "but keep him out of my sight."

Five minutes later the ropes were cut away from me and I was lifted out of the hold, put in a bunk in the "forecastle" (pronounced "fo'c'sle"), where the sailors lived, and covered with heavy sea blankets. I closed my eyes and tumbled into sleep.

For a whole week I rested in that bed, enjoying the daylight, the fresh sea wind that came in through a porthole, and the company of the sailors. They were a rough crowd but they treated me with kindness. Even though they led a wild and lawless life out on the oceans, there was something decent about them. The money that had been in my pockets was missing when I woke up, but within a few days two-thirds of it had been returned to me. One of the sailors told me that my money had been divided between them by the captain, to pay for their silence in my kidnapping. But most of them felt sorry for me, and so they wanted to give it back.

I discovered that I was being carried to the tobacco plantations in the American state of Carolina. My fiend of an uncle had made a bargain with the captain that he could sell me into slavery. With the risks of disease and the backbreaking work I would be forced to do, it was not expected that I would survive for long. My uncle had outfoxed me, and would keep the estate of the Shaws that was rightfully mine.

Ransome came in now and again to see how I was recovering. He worked and slept in the "roundhouse", the officers' quarters. Each time he visited he complained about the violence of the first mate, Mr. Shaun, who was drunk all day, from "waking to sleeping". Ransome told me that the other mate, Mr. Riach, to whom I owed my life, was another heavy drinker, but when he was drunk he "wouldn't hurt a fly".

I tried my best to help Ransome, but he didn't listen to the advice I gave him, to leave the ship as soon as he could. Years of hardship and cruelty on the world's oceans had unsettled his mind. He started talking and singing to himself and the crew became nervous around him.

All through that week we were battling a gale and the sailors were busy at their work. I lay on my bunk, listening to their shouts and the remorseless battering of the waves. The ship seemed a terrible place to me, but when I thought of my final destination I wondered if I might soon look back on this time with longing.

One night, around midnight, a man from the deck watch came down to collect his jacket and I could hear the other sailors whispering with him.

"Shaun has done for him now," I heard one of them mutter. My heart ached inside me. There was no need to guess the name of the victim. The door of the forecastle was pulled back suddenly and the captain entered, looking around him as though searching for someone.

"Balfour," he growled. "You're to take over in the roundhouse. Ransome will be swapping bunks with you."

Behind him, two sailors came in with Ransome lying stretched across their arms. At that moment, the ship lurched on a freak wave and the lantern swung around to reveal Ransome's face. His skin was white as fresh snow and the features were contorted in a terrible grimace of pain. I jumped out of my bunk and shoved my way past the sailors and their burden at the door.

Standing six feet above the deck, the roundhouse was a square room with a small kitchen, a table and two bunks. One of these was for the captain, the other for whichever mate wasn't on duty on deck.

The walls were lined with lockers for the ship's provisions and there was a hatch in the middle of the floor that opened into a "below-decks" store-room. Most of the food and drink was stored here, as well as all the firearms and ammunition. On two sides of the room there were doors opening onto the deck, and there was a small side-window and a skylight in the roof, to let the daylight in. At night there was always a lamp standing on the table.

When I entered, cautiously peering around the door, the lamp gave off a dull glow and I could just make out the dark shape of Mr. Shaun sitting at the table, staring straight ahead of him at a bottle of brandy. He made no sign that he had noticed me, and it was the same when the captain and Mr. Riach joined us a minute later.

The two men exchanged a glance which I read as meaning the cabin boy was dead, then we all stared at the man at the table, who looked as though he was in a trance. Suddenly he stretched his hand out for the brandy bottle, but Mr. Riach stepped forward and grabbed it.

"There's been enough of that tonight," he shouted and, leaning out through the open door behind him, tossed the bottle into the sea. The chief mate jumped up from the table and charged at Mr. Riach, but the captain stepped between them.

"Sit down," he yelled at Mr. Shaun. "You've murdered the boy, you drunken swine."

The killer fell back into his chair and rubbed his face with his hands. "Well, he brought me a dirty cup," he muttered.

The three of us looked at each other, astounded by these words, then the captain stepped over to Mr. Shaun and led him over to his bunk. The murderer let out a sob like a child, then took off his sea boots and climbing onto the bed, rolled his face to the cabin wall.

The captain came back to us and herded us out onto the deck. "The boy went overboard," he whispered.

Riach and I stared at him in silence.

"He drowned, you understand?" the captain continued. "Now, I need a drink. What made you throw that bottle of good brandy away, Mr. Riach? Fetch me another, Davie." He handed me a key and directed me to one of the cupboards. "And bring a cup for Mr. Riach," he called after me. "It is an ugly thing he has seen this evening. A drink will help him forget it."

These were the men I was ordered to serve until we reached the slave plantations of America. I brought them food and brandy (and it was mostly brandy) whenever they called for it, night and day, storm or calm. I slept on the roundhouse floor, huddled under a coarse wool blanket in the breeze from the two sea-doors. I was the galley slave; running messages, making the porridge and pouring their drinks. The only good thing about my new job was that my masters were never rough or angry with me. I believe the murder of Ransome had softened them a little, and they were always patient and forgiving, no matter what mistakes I made.

In spite of the hard work, I came to enjoy the small pleasures of life in the roundhouse. There was always plenty to eat and the work wasn't too arduous. Mr. Riach used to tell me fantastic stories about his past. Even the captain was in a garrulous mood now and again, describing the exotic countries he had visited in his thirty years at sea. But always at the back of my mind was the prospect of slavery in the tobacco fields that awaited me. Thinking of this fate, my heart sank lower and lower, and I would stare out to the horizon, wondering how I might be saved.

One morning the captain came in, reeking of whisky, and told me to fetch his sea charts. When I returned the two mates were standing talking with him in hushed voices.

"I believe we made less than two miles yesterday," muttered the captain.

"By my reckoning," interrupted Mr. Riach, "we've gone *back* a mile."

The ship had been fighting heavy winds since the start of the voyage. Not being familiar with the sea, I'd thought this was how all sailing was done. Now I realized that if the wind was blowing against us, our progress must be correspondingly slow.

The captain spread the charts across the table and the three men pored over them. They were so intent on studying the maps they didn't remember to send me out of the room on some errand (as was usual, when they had an officer's meeting). Being curious, I crept closer, to take a look.

After three weeks at sea, I had believed we must be halfway across the Atlantic Ocean by now. But as I looked at the chart I thought I recognized the shape of Scotland. The captain was pointing to a square at the very top of a block of land, and I could see the lettering:

We were only a few miles off the Highlands of my own country. I slipped out onto the deck. Across the choppy waters I could see a green smudge of land. It was Scotland. If we were still so close, perhaps I was wrong to give up my hopes of escaping this watery prison.

That afternoon a thick, wet fog came down around the ship. The captain set watches of sailors to listen out for "breakers", and although I didn't understand this term, I felt there was some danger in the air.

It was ten o'clock and I was serving dinner, when there was a great crash and the ship rocked to one side, sending the plates clattering to the floor.

"We're on the rocks," screamed Mr. Riach.

"No, sir," said the captain calmly. "The rocks are far worse than that. I believe we've rammed another ship."

The captain was right. The *Covenant* had sliced through a small boat, and the crew were all lost except for one man. The survivor had been sitting in the stern of his boat and seen the prow of the *Covenant* break out of the wall of fog. Knowing that the craft he was in was about to be smashed and sunk, he jumped up and grabbed the long pole, the "bowsprit", that protrudes from the front of the ship, and pulled himself aboard.

I had seen the sailors on the *Covenant* climbing in the masts, and respected their agility. But to jump from one moving ship to another was an incredible feat, requiring extraordinary strength and daring. Yet,

when the man was led up to the roundhouse to meet the captain, he looked as calm and cool as though he'd been woken from an afternoon nap.

He was the same height as I was, but he was stocky and nimble as a goat. His face was sunburned and scarred, and he had bright, piercing eyes. It was clear he took great pride in his dress, for he wore a jacket decorated with silver buttons and lace, a feathered hat and fine velvet trousers. After he had removed his hat, he took out two silver-handled pistols and laid them on the table. Glinting by his side was a wide sword, hanging from a shoulder belt.

"My apologies, sir," the captain began, "for your boat."

"Save them for my men," snapped the stranger, "sent to the bottom of the sea."

"Were they Frenchmen, by any chance?" the captain asked with a sly look.

Our visitor had his hands on the pistols in a flash. "Is that my welcome aboard then?" he shouted. "What do you know about France?"

"Don't be so hasty," said the captain in a soothing voice. "I've docked in that country and I recognize French clothes. I know there are some Scotsmen who are safer in France than they are in their own land, but that doesn't mean I bear them any harm."

I had heard stories from my father about the lawless Scottish rebels, members of the fierce Highland clans who did not want the English army in our country, but I had never encountered one before.

For decades, our country had been divided by religion. As I understood it, the clans and their French allies were Catholics. Five years earlier, they had staged an uprising against King George. They wanted to see a Catholic monarch, Bonnie Prince Charlie, on the throne. It had been a long and violent revolt, only ending at the terrible Battle of Culloden, when the army of the clans was crushed.

"Rebel or not," said the stranger with a smile, "I am an honest gentleman. It's true that I've had an argument or two with the redcoats in my time. And I am heading for France. I was out here looking for a French ship that must have missed us in the fog. It's a shame you didn't do the same."

"I have already given you my apology," said the captain sternly.

"You could give me more than that," replied the stranger, resting his pistols on the table once more.

"I am listening," said the captain.

"If you could take me where I was heading, before your interruption, I would reward you for the inconvenience."

"Landing you in France," boomed the captain. "is out of the question. We're bound for America. But I might be willing to return you to the Scottish coast. It would depend on what you have to offer, of course."

The stranger reached inside his jacket and took a leather money-belt from under his shirt. "Thirty pounds from this purse," he whispered, "if you can land me on the shore, away from any redcoat patrols."

The captain shrugged his shoulders. "If I was caught with you on board they might charge me as an accomplice. I wouldn't risk my captain's licence for less than sixty pounds."

"The money's not mine to squander," replied the stranger angrily. "It belongs to my chieftain. I collected it from his loyal clan members, to help support him in the land where he lives in exile. It's my duty to deliver it, not waste it all on saving my own skin. I can afford thirty pounds, and no more."

"It might be safer for me," whispered the captain craftily, "to hand you over to the soldiers."

"I know what you're thinking," answered the stranger. "You think a pile of coins from my purse could be yours as a reward. But you're wrong. I've already told you, my chieftain is in exile in France. His estate has been occupied by King George's troops and tax collectors. The clan members give me whatever money they can spare or steal from the authorities, and I carry it back to France. How much of it do you think the English tax collectors would hand over to you?"

"You have a point there," admitted the captain. "Well then, I'll stick with your offer. Thirty pounds it is, for safe passage to the mainland."

They shook hands and then the captain stepped out of the room, rather in a hurry, I thought.

"What about a drink, cabin boy?" the stranger barked at me. "If I'm paying thirty pounds for the journey, I think the captain can spare me a bottle."

I nodded my head and told him I would go and

ask for the key to the liquor cabinet.

The fog was swirling over the decks now, so thick I couldn't see my own feet. I followed the ropes down the side of the ship until I came to a huddle of men. The words I overheard coming out of that white blur made me stop in my tracks.

"We should trick him out of the roundhouse."

"No, Mr. Riach," snapped the captain's gruff voice. "Trapped in there he doesn't have room to use his sword properly. We'll start talking with him and then pin his arms, or rush him from both sides of the cabin and grab him before he can draw."

Standing there in the thick fog, listening to these treacherous, greedy voices, I decided that I might have more in common with the rebel in the roundhouse than I did with the ship's crew. Hearing their words reminded me how they'd kidnapped me and were planning to sell me into slavery. But was it possible that they were loyal subjects to King George? I needed to know if they were trying to protect the king by seizing the rebel, or if they were a ship of thieves, out for the stranger's gold, as I suspected.

"Captain," I cried out. "The gentleman wants a bottle from the cabinet. Will you give me the key?"

The men jumped around and dragged me into their circle.

"Here's our chance to get the firearms," hissed Mr. Riach.

"Yes, Davie," said the captain excitedly, "this

Highland rebel is a danger to my ship, and an enemy to our king. You'll help us capture him, won't you."

"Of course, sir," I cried. And I remembered the soft, encouraging voice of the captain on the quayside at Queensferry. I would not be taken in by it a second time.

"The problem, Davie," he whispered, his hand resting on my shoulder as though we were shipmates, "is that all our firearms are locked in the roundhouse, right under the rebel's nose. If I, or one of the officers, was to go in and take one from the chest, he'd be suspicious. But he won't be watching the cabin boy for tricks. If you could slip one or two pistols into your jacket without him seeing, then smuggle them out to us, well, you can count on me as a friend when we get to Carolina."

At this point Mr. Riach leaned over and whispered into the captain's ear.

"Of, course," said the captain, turning away from his officer, "I give you my word that you'll get a fair share of the stranger's gold. There must be hundreds of pounds in that money belt of his, and we mean to take it."

"I'll do it, sir," I told him, trying not to show my disgust. It was obvious they weren't motivated by a sense of duty, but by plain criminal greed. The captain passed me the key and I started creeping back toward the roundhouse.

I walked straight up to the rebel and put my hand on his shoulder.

"Do you want to be killed?" I asked him. His hand was on his sword instantly.

"They're all killers on this ship," I went on. "They've murdered a boy already, and you're next."

"And what are you?" he demanded.

"I'm not one of them. I'm not a thief or a murderer."

"Will you stand with me then?"

"I will. But I don't see what chance we have against a whole ship's company."

"If you're brave enough," he said, "you always have a chance." He sat down by the table and started checking his pistols. "What is your name?" he asked, not looking up at me.

"David Balfour," I replied. And then, thinking this man in his fancy clothes might be impressed by my full title, I added, "Of Shaws." He stood up and faced me.

"I am from the Stewart clan. They call me Alan Breck," he said proudly, "and that's all there is. I don't own any estates, so I don't hang another word onto the end of my name. I don't need to."

I was surprised at his rebuke, and felt a little embarrassed for bragging about my title. But, before I could say anything, he was stalking around the roundhouse, examining it for weak spots.

The room we were in was built to withstand the pounding of the Atlantic storms. Only the two side doors and the skylight were big enough to let a man enter, and these openings all had heavy, sliding panels which could be locked shut, with hooks mounted on the wall. I locked the door behind me and then stepped towards the other door that stood open onto the deck, but Alan put his hand up.

"David," he said with a chuckle, "if I may call you that, I seem to have forgotten the name of your landed estate..."

"I don't think this is the right time for your mockery," I said, bristling slightly. "You can call me David."

"That open door," he said, still smiling, "is the best protection for us."

"Don't we need it shut and locked?" I cried.

"As long as the door remains open, our enemies will come through it. That means they have to face me."

I was starting to wonder if Alan Breck was the right man to side with, and whether I'd stand a better chance swimming across the open sea to the mainland. And then I remembered I couldn't swim, and I gulped.

"Are you that good a swordsman?" I asked him.

"I am. But it's better to fight ten men coming in a straight line than ten men spread out all around you. The open door will draw them in, in file. Now, can you load a pistol?"

I nodded my head.

"If I was a gentleman with estates, I'd rather load pistols than work as a cabin boy," he said with a smirk.

"I am happy to load," I said, again annoyed by his sarcasm.

"Good, set us up a pile of them."

Then he unbuckled his great sword and began slicing it through the air. "This little room cramps my style, David," he shouted, jabbing the point of the sword toward the door. "But we'll have to make do with it."

Then he rested the weapon on the table next to me.

"We must have a conference of war," he said softly. "How many men does the captain have?"

"Fifteen," I answered. "There's a strongbox full of cutlasses in the forecastle but we have all the firearms." My voice was cracking and I realized my throat was dry. Suddenly, I thought about the men who would be crashing through the open door at any moment, ready to kill us.

"Be brave," whispered Alan, noticing that my nerve was weakening. "I'll defend the open door. You must protect my back."

"What about the other door? They might break it in."

"Once you've finished loading the pistols, take a cutlass from the rack on the wall and climb up on the top bunk. There's a window you can shoot the pistols through if they try to attack on that side."

"But if I'm watching the door," I mumbled nervously, "how can I keep an eye on the skylight above me?"

"Use your ears," he answered, with a smile. "What will they hear?"

"The sound of breaking glass?"

"Good, Davie, go to the top of the class."

Battle Stations

There was a scraping sound at the door and we looked over to see the sour face of the captain. Alan jumped up from the table and pointed his sword in his direction.

"A naked sword?" growled the captain. "What kind of thanks is that, for all my hospitality?"

"See this sword?" laughed Alan. "This sword's slashed more heads off redcoats than you have toes on your feet. Call up your rotten crew and start the fight. The sooner we begin, the sooner you'll feel this steel in your belly."

The captain didn't answer this challenge, but looked over at me with a dark look. "I thought you'd been gone a long time," he hissed. "I'll remember this, Davie," and then he was gone.

"Get ready," cried Alan. "Keep a steady hand," he chuckled, "and you may keep your head."

I climbed up to the top bunk with a pile of pistols and a rusty cutlass. Then I peered out of a small window into the fog and gloom that hung around the ship. The sea was calm and there was no wind, so I could hear the muttering of voices, a little further along the deck.

"They're making plans," I said to Alan, my voice shaking. I realized my heart was racing and my eyes blurry. I kept rubbing them, so I could keep my vigil on the clear patch of deck below the window. But with every second that passed I grew more nervous, and I longed for the battle to start so this terrible waiting could be over.

I soon got my wish. There was a roar and the sound of feet thumping on the deck, then a shout from Alan. I looked over my shoulder and saw him slashing at Mr. Shaun in the doorway. Their swords were sparking in the lamplight, and there was a mob of men pushing behind the mate, trying to get into the room.

"He's the one who killed the cabin boy," I screamed.

"Get back to your post," yelled Alan, and just as I turned back to the window I saw him sink his great sword into the first mate's chest.

It was a good job I turned then, because when I looked out onto the deck I saw a huddle of men dragging a thick post up to the door below me. They lined up on either side of the post and got ready to use it as a battering ram.

I had never fired a pistol before in my life, but with trembling fingers I pointed the steel barrel towards the shuffling group, cried out, "Take that," and pulled the trigger. There was a great flash and a "boom" that made my ears ring and I watched one of the men stagger back, clutching at his arm. The others halted with the ram. Before they had time to understand, I fired another shot over their heads. With my third shot our attackers dropped their ram and were sprinting off into the fog.

I fell back, exhausted, across the bunk. The whole room was full of clouds of acrid smoke from the gunpowder, and my ears were hissing as though I stood on the banks of a mighty river. I glanced down at Alan, his figure wrapped in wreaths of the swirling smoke. He was still in the same position, guarding the door, but now his sword was smeared with blood, from tip to hilt. He arced the blade through the air and I saw his face flushed with triumph, as though he considered himself an invincible warrior. At his feet, Mr. Shaun was sunk to his hands and knees. Blood gushed from his mouth and he was sinking lower and lower, his face white as Ransome's the night he died.

As I watched, two men appeared at the door. They grabbed the mate by his heels and dragged him out to the deck. Alan waited to make sure they had all gone, then turned to me and slapped a bloody fist down on my shoulder.

"How many did you get?" he shouted.

"I winged one, and it might have been the captain."

"Good work, Davie. But it's not over yet. That was only the first course of the feast. They'll soon be back for more. To your station," he ordered.

I went back to my perch and carefully loaded the three pistols I'd fired. During the fighting there'd been no time to think. But as soon as I started watching the deck again, and waiting to see what they'd try next, the fear returned. The thought of their razor-sharp cutlasses and the captain's menacing look made me shiver. When I heard steps out on the deck, and the brush of a man's jacket against the wall of the roundhouse, I was so nervous I wanted to scream. Then I heard a footstep on the roof above my head.

There was a single high-pitched note on a sea pipe. That must have been their signal to attack. I saw a knot of men crowding at the door. That moment, the glass of the skylight exploded into a thousand pieces. One of the sailors crashed through and landed on the boards below me. At once I leaned down and put the muzzle of a pistol to his back, but as soon as

I felt him twitch at the touch of it, my courage vanished. It would have been easier to fly away on the wind than pull the trigger.

The man had dropped his cutlass when he'd landed but now he snatched it up and I saw him swinging it around in the direction of my throat. There was no time to wonder if I was doing the right thing. In a fraction of a second, I knew that if I hesitated, he wouldn't. I shot him in the stomach.

I felt a blow to the side of my head and looked around to see a foot dangling from the skylight. Another man was trying to force his way in, and this time I didn't pause. I snatched up another pistol and shot him in the thigh. He screamed in pain and crashed down onto the wriggling body of his comrade. As his hand reached for his cutlass, I pushed a pistol against his chest and fired.

I was so dazed and horrified by the blood and noise all around me, for a few seconds I couldn't move. But then I heard Alan calling out for me. His sword danced in the air against a flurry of cutlasses, jabbing at him from the doorway. The gang of sailors were driving him back into the room, about to rush in and cut us down. It looked as though we were finished, but I wasn't ready to give up without a fight. I grabbed my cutlass, dropped to the floor, and joined the sword fight.

But Alan was braver than I'd realized. He charged at the wall of attackers, roaring and huffing like a wild bull. The sailors broke ranks and fled, with Alan in pursuit. His sword flashed among their retreating bodies, and with each flash there was the scream of a man, cut and bleeding. He drove them out onto the deck and herded them away from the roundhouse like a sheep dog chasing sheep.

But he was as cautious as he was brave, and he didn't go too far from the roundhouse. After he'd rolled the bodies of the dead sailors out of our room, he watched from the doorway for a few minutes and then, satisfied there would be no sudden counter-attack, he stepped into the room and rested his sword on the table.

"Come into my arms," he yelled. And he embraced me, with kisses on both cheeks. "Am I not a great warrior?" he yelled, and I nodded my head and smiled. "And you too, Davie, of Shaws," he added, after a pause, "you're not a bad warrior yourself."

We shared watches for the rest of that night, and there were no more raids. So many of the crew were dead or injured, the ship rolled and dropped on the tide with no one to guide her or tend to the sails. When the morning sun at last filled the roundhouse with its golden light, I stepped out onto the deck and saw a cloud of gulls sweeping around our masts. We were even closer to the shores of Scotland than we'd been the day before. I could almost smell the heather.

At six o'clock we sat down to breakfast. I can't say I had much appetite for the meal; the floor was sticky with blood and covered in broken glass. But we had the best food on the ship – and all the wine and brandy. What pleased me most was to think of Mr. Riach and the captain, the two thirstiest men ever to come out of Scotland, shut in the forecastle with nothing but biscuits and cold water.

"That's good," smiled Alan when I'd told him what heavy drinkers they were. "It means they'll want to talk. You can keep a man from fighting, but never from his bottle."

We talked as though we were friends, and I remembered what it was like to be among good people again. Despite his ferocity when wielding the sword, Alan was a tender and generous man. While we were chatting, he took a knife from the table, cut off one of the silver buttons from his jacket and handed it to me.

"They were my father's," he said proudly. "Wherever you go and show that button, the friends of Alan Breck will come to aid you."

He said this as though he was a king talking to his army generals. Much as I admired his courage I was stunned by his vanity. After breakfast he rummaged around in the chests for a clothes brush, then proceeded to tend to his cloak and jacket, brushing away at the bloodstains. But when I saw how carefully he plucked out the threads where the cut button had been, I realized how valuable this gift had been to him.

Alan was still tending to his clothes when Mr. Riach hailed us from the deck, asking for a "parley".

I climbed up through the holed skylight with a pistol in one hand, and sat on the roof of the roundhouse with a bold look on my face, though in truth I was scared of cutting myself on the broken glass. Mr. Riach came over and stood on a coil of rope so his chin was level with the roof. We stared at each other in silence. He had a bloody cheek and he looked terribly weary.

"This is a bad business," he sighed.

"We didn't ask for it," I replied.

"The captain wants a meeting with your new friend."

"Another trick?" I snapped.

"We're too far gone for any more tricks. The captain gave me his word there'd be none. We just want the rebel off the ship."

I hopped down through the skylight and consulted with Alan. All the time, on the other side of the roundhouse wall, Mr. Riach was pleading with me for a sip of brandy. At last I brought him a cupful, and the message that we would listen to the captain. He sipped at the drink as though it was medicine, and then he carried the rest off to his thirsty superior.

Ten minutes later the captain hobbled over to the roundhouse door and stood there with his arm in a sling, pale-faced and red-eyed. He looked so old after the hardships of the previous day, I almost felt sorry for him. Alan immediately held a pistol to his face.

"I've given you my word, sir," roared the captain.

"We shook hands on your word yesterday," replied

Alan with a snarl.

"Things have changed since then," answered the captain. "You've made a mess of my ship for one thing. Half my crew's dead or maimed, and my first officer's been buried under the waves. I'm bound for the port of Glasgow, where I'll take on new men. You can try your luck with the redcoats," he added with a scowl.

"I'll have a story to tell them," laughed Alan. "How a captain and his fifteen men were whipped in a sword fight, by one man and boy."

Hoseason's haggard face flushed scarlet.

"No," continued Alan. "It won't do. You'll put me ashore as we agreed and then you can sail for Glasgow. If you don't like it then get your men ready for another battle."

"As you should know," hissed the captain, "my first officer is dead. This is a dangerous coast and he was the only man who was familiar with it. We're between the islands and the mainland now. The currents are perilous and a ship this size runs the risk of striking an underwater reef."

"Land me or fight me," demanded Alan.

"I don't like risking my ship," snapped the captain, "and it'll cost me money to waste another day before sailing to Glasgow."

"Unlike you, I don't go back on my word. Thirty pounds if you land me on dry ground."

"Could you pilot the ship?" asked the captain craftily.

"I could try," said Alan. "I've been up and down

this coast a hundred times."

"Very well," said the captain with a frown. "But if we meet a King's ship out on patrol, I still want my money from you."

"If you see a King's ship," laughed Alan, "I'll expect you to sail in the opposite direction, or the gold follows after your first mate."

The captain glowered at us in silence.

"I have a further request," continued Alan. "I'll offer you a bottle of brandy for two buckets of clean water."

At this, the captain's eyes lit up considerably. The deal was agreed and the goods exchanged. We used the water to wash down the soiled roundhouse floor and scrub ourselves clean, while the captain and Mr. Riach were soon howling drunk, and could be heard arguing and cursing in the forecastle.

There followed a day of fair sailing, with a good breeze behind us and the wave-crests glittering in the sun. Alan smoked a pipe of the captain's tobacco and we told each other our stories. I learned a lot about the wild Highland country and the business of the clans and the English forces that had taken control of their lands. Then he listened patiently to my misfortunes, until I mentioned the name of my friend, the minister, Mr. Campbell.

"But I hate all men of that name," he cried.

"Why, Alan," I answered, "he is a good friend to me."

"He may have been to you," he said grudgingly, "but the Campbell clan are at war with my clan, the Stewarts." He smashed his hand down onto the table. "They've tricked us and stolen our land. And they conspire with the English to rob us of the little we have left."

"Perhaps you gave it away to them, in a show of pride," I said angrily. "In the same way you gave me your father's silver button."

"There's no need for mean words, Davie," replied Alan, and I felt guilty that I'd insulted him. "It's true I'm not careful with my money. I inherited that trait from my father. No better man, or swordsman, ever lived. But he was too generous with his fortune and when he died there wasn't enough to feed us. That was how I came to enlist..."

"You joined the English army?" I stammered in surprise.

"I did and it's still a black spot on my character. But I was starving. I soon saw sense and crossed sides."

"So you're a deserter?" I asked him.

"I am, and under punishment of death."

I was silent for a moment. I had always thought of deserters as cowards and rogues, but here was a man I knew to be a brave fighter, and who I already considered a friend. A lot had changed since I'd left Essendean and I realized the simple convictions about "right and wrong" that I'd held in that place might be harder to apply out in the wider world.

"I am sorry, Alan," I muttered. "But you are a rebel fighter, an army deserter and one of the French king's men. Why do you want to go back to Scotland, where they will surely catch you and hang you?"

"Oh," he said casually, "I've been back every year for six years since the uprising. France is a pretty place but I miss my friends and country. I miss the perfume of the heather and the sight of a deer. And I have my duties, of course, recruiting new soldiers for France and collecting the money for my chief, Ardshiel. His clansmen in Scotland have to pay a rent to King George, but they are loyal to their chief. With loyalty, and a little pressure from me, they scrape up a second rent. And I am the man who delivers it." He slapped the money belt at his waist and I heard the clink of the coins.

"They pay two rents, these poor farmers?" I asked. "I call that noble. I'm a supporter of King George, but your clan has my respect, Alan."

"Yes," he sighed. "You're loyal to King George, but at least you can show respect and kindness to others. You call it "noble", the way my people take the food out of their own mouths to give to their chief. But if you were a Campbell, you'd be outraged. You'd want to steal that money for yourself. If you were the Red Fox..."

Alan sat back in his chair, his face dark with fury. The mention of this man's name was enough to silence him with rage.

"Who is... the Red Fox?" I said, scared to ask but too curious not to. Alan leaned toward me and his eyes stared into mine.

"When the clans were decimated by the English, at the Battle of Culloden," he began, his voice barely more than a whisper, "Ardshiel, my chief, had to flee like a deer on the hillside. While we had him hidden, arranging to ship him to his friends in France, the English stripped him of his powers and of his lands. They plucked the weapons from the hands of his clansmen – men who'd borne arms for thirty centuries, Davie – and even made it a crime to wear the Stewart tartan. But they couldn't destroy the love the clan felt for its chief. So we started collecting the second rent. But there was a Campbell, a man with flame-red hair, Colin of Glenure..."

"The Red Fox?" I whispered.

"He got a contract from King George to take the rent from my chief's lands. And when he heard there was a second rent being collected, he was so mad with anger he started gnashing his teeth and pulling at his hair. He was determined that not a penny should reach my chief in France. So he got another contract that said he could put all our farms on the market, to be sold."

"How was he allowed to do that?" I cried.

"He had the King's permission to do anything he liked," thundered Alan. "But the clansmen pooled all their money together and offered to buy the farms themselves, the same farms they already owned. No Campbells came forward with a better price."

"So he was beaten then?"

"The Red Fox doesn't give up so easily, Davie. With the support of the redcoats, he plans to throw my clan off their property. Such a man doesn't deserve to live. If I ever get the Red Fox in my sight, I'll be doing the whole of Scotland a service if I squeeze the trigger."

I tried my best to convince Alan that violence wasn't the way to solve our country's problems but he called me a "Whig" (an insulting term meaning anyone who opposed a Catholic Scotland) and showed every sign of flying into another rage. I thought it best to change the subject.

I learned a few other things about my new friend. He was passionate and fierce, but he had his soft side. He was skilled in all kinds of music and was often humming or whistling a tune to himself. It was the Highland pipes that were his best instrument, he told me. He recited Gaelic poems for me, which sounded beautiful, even though I had no idea what the words meant. He could read in French and English, was a dead shot, and a master of all kinds of swords.

He didn't dwell much on his faults, but few of us do. Perhaps the worst of them was his readiness to get offended and to argue, even over the most trivial matters. I was often spared this argumentative streak of his, because of his respect for me after the battle of the roundhouse. Whether this was because I had fought well myself, or because I had witnessed his own, fearsome powers as a warrior, I couldn't tell.

He had a great respect for courage in other men, but I suspected he admired it most in himself.

The Torran Rocks

In the summertime, in the Highlands of Scotland, the sun lingers so long in the evening sky it doesn't get dark until eleven or twelve o'clock. Even then, it's often bright enough to read a book. It was midnight when the captain popped his head around the roundhouse door, but it was so light I could see the fear stamped across his features.

"My ship's in danger," he cried. "Come out and see if you can pilot."

By the look on his face and the tremor in his voice, we didn't suspect any trickery. We pulled on some coats and stepped out onto the deck.

The wind was blowing hard now, and it was bitterly cold. The coastline was off to the port-side, a black smudge of low hills. The seas were high, but nothing the *Covenant* couldn't handle. I'd seen her surge through storms ten times as rough as this and I began to wonder if the captain might be up to something after all. But then he suddenly pointed to the open water between us and the land.

"Look there," he shouted against the wind.

At first I thought it was a fountain in the middle of the sea. A great jet of foam swelled and then blasted out from the moonlit waters, followed by a low, rumbling roar.

"A reef," cried Alan. "The water's breaking on a reef. But that's fine, man," he scolded the captain, "that landmark will give us our position on the charts. What more do you want?"

"Look again," the captain replied, his eyes staring past us and back out to the sea. I turned and saw another fountain, ahead of us, even closer.

"They're all around us," the captain yelled.

"They are," said Alan, "and I believe they might be the beginning of what the locals call 'The Torran Rocks'."

"The beginning?" cried the captain, in alarm.

"I seem to remember," said Alan, his face twisted in concentration, "there are ten miles of them."

The captain and Mr. Riach stared at one another in horror.

"Is there a way through?" asked the mate.

"I can't be sure," answered Alan, "but I think I was told it's safer to stay close to the land."

"Close to shore, Mr. Riach," ordered the captain. "Change the sail and bring her in. We'll have rocks on one side, and rocks on the other. But we can't turn her around now, so let's see if we can creep through." And then he turned back to Alan and me. "If I'd known about these reefs," he spat, "I wouldn't have carried you for six hundred pounds, never mind thirty," and he stomped off to the prow of his ship.

There were only three sailors fit enough to work in the rigging; the rest lay wounded in the forecastle.

So the captain sent Mr. Riach up the main mast to keep a lookout. At once the mate started calling down changes of course, to avoid the reefs. "Hard to starboard," he called, and the captain threw his weight against the tiller at the stern of the ship, making the whole vessel lurch to the right. Sometimes he called out late, and the glistening black rock of the reefs slid alongside, like a school of sharks waiting for any scraps of food to be thrown from the deck. One reef came so close that, when the water broke on its back, a shower of salt water fell down on the decks in a heavy rain.

The brightness of the night showed us the deadly reefs as clearly as if it had been day. I studied the face of the captain at the stern, thinking an examination of him might tell me what our chances were. His eyes were sparkling and his hands set like steel around the wheel. In the roundhouse battle, the captain and Mr. Riach hadn't fought well, but in their own business as seafaring men they were braver than we were.

The ship was close to the land now and the tide was strong, pushing us toward the rocks along the shore. I watched as the tiller bucked and twisted like a live beast in the churning waters all around us. There was a call from Mr. Riach above: "Clear water ahead."

"You've saved my ship," the captain called to Alan. For a moment we thought we were safe, but then there was a desperate scream from the mate: "Reef on the port side."

At that second, the tide twisted the ship around

and the sails were loose and flapping, out of the wind. Without the wind to help push us forward, the ship lurched again to the port-side and we struck the rocks with such a crunch that we were all thrown across the deck.

I sprang to my feet and looked over the side. There was the black mound of an island between us and the coast, and all around stretched the moon-white sea. But then the tide swelled beneath us and I could hear the bottom of the ship grating and cracking on the reef. The next second the waters dropped and a wave came right across the deck, knocking me onto my back again. The sails were clapping and snapping above my head, and the wind and water roared on every side, but that was not the worst noise I heard. From the forecastle there were screams and groans, as the men who were too badly wounded to walk realized we were on the rocks and called out to us to save them.

The captain didn't move from the tiller. His eyes were glazed and dull and I could hear him muttering something to himself, sobbing with pain each time he heard his beloved ship rolling back across the reef, grinding her mighty timbers to splinters.

I turned to Alan who was surveying the distant coast, "Where are we?" I screamed.

He gave me a dismal look. "In the land of the Campbells," was all he would say.

And then there was another terrible cry, from one of the sailors: "Hold on for your lives."

It was no ordinary shout and no ordinary wave

that surged across the deck, tearing the skiff from her mooring ropes and casting me over the side and into the cold blackness of the sea.

I went down and drank a gallon, then I bobbed up again, got a glimpse of the moon and was pulled down again. They say a man sinks the third time for good. But I must be made differently, because I went up and down like a yo-yo, spitting out water and choking and coughing, and not sure which way was up or down.

At last I winded myself, knocking into a pole of wood from the ship, the same pole the crew had carried up from the hold to use as a battering ram. It floated and I clung onto it with all my strength.

By the time I looked around I saw the ship about a mile off and was shocked that I'd drifted so far. My attempts to hail her were swallowed in the wind.

I started to feel the cold and wondered if I'd freeze to death instead of drowning. But I discovered that I could kick with my legs and push the pole through the water towards the land. After an hour of this, I felt a sandy floor beneath my feet, and dragged myself out of the surf. Aching with exhaustion and pain, I curled into a ball on the beach, and stared up at the stars.

Castaway

The next four days were the most miserable of all my adventure. After scouting around all morning, I realized I was on the island I'd glimpsed from the reef, cut off from the coast by half a mile of impassable, open water. From a hilltop on the south side of the isle I could see a distant village on the mainland. During the day I watched the trails of smoke rising from the cottage chimneys, and at night I could make out their lamps, glinting in the dark. But the village might as well have been on the moon, for all the help it could give to me.

My hunger was terrible. I would have starved but I remembered that shellfish could be eaten. Wading out to the shoreline rocks, I dislodged a pocketful of limpets with a stone. Back on the beach I sucked them out of their shells, raw, salty and cold. The feel of them slipping down my throat was revolting but they eased the hunger.

By the third day I was in a pitiful state. My clothes were starting to rot and fray, my hands were wrinkled and soft from the continual damp, my throat was sore and just the sight of another squidgy limpet was enough to make me retch. As if this wasn't bad enough, I discovered that most of my pound coins had slipped through a hole in my jacket pocket. From my fortune of twenty pounds, I now had three remaining. I slapped my brow at the thought of this loss. But there was worse to come.

During a rare burst of sunshine, I climbed to the top of the hill and stretched myself out, to try to dry my clothes. All of a sudden a fishing boat turned around the headland, so close I could see the two men at the sails and their flaming red hair.

I tore down the hill, shouting and pleading for them to rescue me. I could hear them laughing and mocking me in a language I thought must be Gaelic. The boat kept going, beyond the rocks and out to sea.

For twenty minutes I hurled insults after them. At first I couldn't believe their wickedness to another human being, and then I wondered if they had heard my English tongue and decided I wasn't worth saving. I cursed the squabbles and politics of my country, that could make the way a person talked or looked a reason to hate him.

On the fourth day I felt weak and sick but the sun was shining, so I hauled myself up the hill again, to try to warm my bones. As soon as I'd scrambled up there, I spied a boat coming back in from the sea.

They sailed to within fifty yards of the shore but came no further. I recognized it as the same boat, with the same two men, but now they were joined by a third, who was taller and wore more elegant clothes. I ran down the hill to call to them.

The tall man stood up in the bobbing boat and spoke at length, in what I assumed was Gaelic, but it could have been Greek or Chinese for all I understood of it. He kept pointing toward the north of my island.

"Come in and get me," I yelled.

"Oh, you're English," he shouted, and they all started laughing raucously. "We can't come any closer because of the rocks. But if you watch the tide..."

"Tide?" I muttered to myself.

"The tide comes in once a day." With that the fishermen put their sails up and waved a good-bye to me, still roaring with laughter. I stood there, puzzled for a minute. Then my mouth fell open and I started sprinting across the heather.

When I rounded the island to reach the north coast, I saw that the wide channel of water (always a choppy and imposing stretch of sea every time I'd looked before) had been drained by an ebbing tide. I could wade the half-mile across to the other shore, in water below my knees. When I reached the beach I fell down and kissed the sand.

My prison was a tidal islet, that could be reached at low tide every twenty-four hours. If I hadn't wasted so much time pitying myself, and instead sat down and worked through the problem in my head, I wouldn't have spent more than a day on that island. It was no surprise the fishermen had laughed at me. I must have looked a strange sight, hopping around on the rocks and waving my arms. Indeed, I should be grateful to these men for coming back to check on me, and explaining about the tidal channel.

If it hadn't been for them, my bones might still be lying on that bleak island, and all because of my own stupidity.

The Boy with the Silver Button

The first house I came across was a decrepit hut of loose stones with a turf roof. An old gentlemen sat on a mound of dirt before it, puffing on a pipe.

His English was scanty, but he explained that my shipmates had landed safely and arrived at the same house, three days ago.

"Was there one of them," I inquired, "who was dressed like a gentleman?"

He told me they all wore rough coats except the first man, who had come alone, an hour before the others, and who wasn't dressed like "a man who lives on the sea". I breathed a sigh of relief. Alan was safe. And then the old man clapped his hand to his forehead, and cried out: "Are you the boy with the silver button?"

"Yes I am," I replied in surprise, and I produced it for him to inspect.

"I have a message for you," he whispered. "You are to follow your friend to his own part of the country, by way of Torosay."

He then listened politely to my embarrassing tale of being captive on the island, and gave me a hearty meal and a bed for the night. I left him the next morning with my faith fully restored in the kindness of strangers.

"If these are the wild highlanders," I thought to myself, "I wish my own Lowland people were a bit wilder."

The old man had told me I was on the Isle of Mull, and it was a rugged, trackless and boggy place that I tramped across that afternoon.

It was around eight o'clock when I came down to a lone house in a valley, and knocked on its door to ask for directions and inquire for a bed for the night. But it was only by holding one of my gleaming gold coins in the air that the scraggy owner would give me admittance. For five shillings he agreed to give me a night's lodgings and point me in the right direction for Torosay.

Next morning, I overtook a great, shuffling man on the track. He was feeling before him with a staff and told me he was a "holy teacher". His blindness and religious faith should have put me at ease, but there was something sinister about his face; it was all scarred and broken and his nose twitched like an animal sniffing out its prey. I kept my distance.

At one point in the path he had to step down into a dip, and glancing across at his huge shape I saw the steel butt of a pistol sticking out from under his coat lapel. Alan had told me that if you were caught by the redcoats carrying a gun, it meant a fine of fifteen pounds for the first time and transportation to the penal colonies for the second. Aside from this risk, it baffled me that a pistol would be much use to a religious man, let alone one who was blind.

"Am I on the right road for Torosay?" I asked him, politely.

"Are you seeking a guide?" he cackled. "I could offer my services as one... if you have any money to offer."

"It seems unusual to have a blind man for a guide."

He pounded the ground with his heavy stick. "This is my eye," he roared. "It's sharp as the eye of an eagle. My memory is finer than any map. On the Isle of Mull I know every rock and heather bush along the track. See now," he cried, casting around with his staff to check his exact location on the path, "down to my right is a stream, and at the head of it is a small hill with a rock balanced on top. At the foot of the hill is the path to Torosay."

"You've described it all," I told him, my voice betraying my wonder, "exactly as it appears."

"That's nothing," he snorted. "Before guns were banned, I was a bit of a marksman. If you had a pistol on you now," he leered, "I could give you a little demonstration."

I told him I was unarmed, and doubled the distance between us on the road. All the time we were walking, the sun was glinting on the steel butt of his pistol, but luckily for me he must have thought it was safely concealed under his jacket.

He began to question me, and all his questions seemed to relate to money. Was I a rich man? (I suppose in those parts I was.) Did I have enough coins on me to change a five shilling piece he had in his purse? By now we were walking on a wide cattle-track. While he edged closer to me all the time, I ducked away. An ignorant observer would have thought we were enjoying some elaborate Highland dance. At last his temper flared up. He started muttering profanities in Gaelic and striking out for my legs with his long staff.

"I think it's time our ways parted," I told him. "I *do* have a pistol in my pocket," I lied, "and I know you carry one. You can take the track to the left and I'll go right, and if you touch that pistol handle I'll blow your brains out."

He swore a terrible oath and stormed off. I watched him striding across the countryside, sweeping his staff before him, and once he was out of my sight I took the path for Torosay.

After this I decided to be more careful who I asked for my directions.

Torosay was a grubby little town on the sea, that looked across to the coast of mainland Scotland. The ferry didn't sail until morning but I found a comfortable inn with a friendly landlord and we sat up all night drinking punch, as seemed to be the custom of the locals.

When I mentioned the wandering bandit I had encountered he looked shocked. "You were lucky to have survived," he whispered. "His name is Duncan Mackiegh and he can aim his pistol by listening to your breathing. There are charges of robbery, and even murder, against him."

"The best thing was," I said, perhaps a little tipsy from the punch, "he claimed to be a holy man."

"And so he is," answered my host. "He has all the credentials. You never know what kind of folk you'll come across," he warned me, wagging his finger, "when you go hiking in the Highlands."

There is a regular ferry between Torosay and Kinlochaline on the mainland. Both towns are in the country of the Macleans, and the voyagers who crossed on the ferry with me were all of that clan. The captain's name was Neil Macrob. I knew that the Macrobs were allies of Alan's clan, so I was anxious to have a private word with him, as soon as we docked. Once the ferry was moored, I waited until the captain was alone before I approached him. "I am seeking somebody," I whispered. "Alan Breck is his name." Like a fool, instead of showing him the silver button, I offered him a shilling.

"I am offended by you, sir," he cried, backing away from me. "Are you offering me your money to betray a friend?"

I quickly showed him the button.

"Well, that changes things," he said, his voice softening. "I do have a message for you. But take my advice in the future. Never mention Alan's name to strangers, and never offer a Highland gentleman your dirty English money."

In my haste I had insulted this man and I felt shamefaced and stupid as I listened to his message. Alan wanted me to spend the night in the town at an inn, then travel to a town called Ardgour and rest in the house of "John of the Claymore". Then I was to ride two ferries around Linnhe Loch to reach the entrance of Loch Leven, and ask my way to the house of "James of the Glens". There is a lot of ferrying to be done when you travel in the Highlands; the sea runs inland through great channels called lochs, like deep grooves between the mountains.

The next morning I set off early and soon caught up with a short, quiet man, dressed in the tunic of a minister, who was staring intently at the pages of a book. His name was Henderland, he told me, and he was a missionary from the Edinburgh church. His soft, Lowland accent was sweet music to my ears. It had been a while since I'd spoken with a fellow lowlander. We shared another bond, as he had read some of the religious writings of my friend, Mr. Campbell of Essendean. Indeed, the book he was carrying was one of them.

He told me of his work with the highlanders and how they suffered with the cruel laws that had been passed by the English parliament. I remembered my vow to be more careful with those I met on the road and didn't go into any details about my journey, saying only that I was voyaging to "meet a friend". But Henderland struck me as quite neutral in his politics, and happy to discuss any topic, and so I decided it would be safe to ask him about the Red Fox.

"Yes, it's a bad business," he sighed. "He's determined to stop any money from getting out of the country. I've no idea where the tenants find the money to pay the second rent, for many of them are so poor they're starving. They're loyal to their chief, but some say they're also given "heavy-handed" encouragement. James of the Glens is half-brother to the chief, and he drives the tenants hard. Then there's the man they call Alan Breck..."

"Ah," I cried, "and what do they say about him?"

"He's a bold and desperate character and travels as lightly as the wind. He's what I call a heather-cat, he's so hard to track down. They say he's James' right-hand man, and has a reputation for violence. Perhaps he encourages the tenants to pay by holding a blade to their throats."

"Do you know that for a fact?" I asked him.

"No, it is only one of the stories that I hear."

"I don't wish to hear stories about the characters of men, if those stories later turn out to be false."

At first his face was stern and I wasn't sure if I had annoyed him, but then he cried, "Well said," and smiled at me. "I've also heard some fine stories about Alan Breck," he continued, "things that make me almost respect him. These are strange times indeed in our country, and we must be careful about judging a man too quickly."

"What else do you know about the Red Fox?" I resumed.

"The first Appin tenants," he replied sadly, "are being evicted in the morning. It's a reckless thing to do."

"You think the Appin clan will fight?"

"I think," he said carefully, "the Red Fox is poking his head into a nest of bees."

We spoke all day about books and the Lowlands and our friend Mr. Campbell, and when Henderland noticed the sun beginning to sink in the west, he invited me to stay with him. His house was on the shore of the very loch I must cross the following day, and because I enjoyed his company so much (and was uncertain where I would find the mysterious John of the Claymore), I said I would be delighted.

I Meet the Red Fox

After the best night's sleep I'd had for weeks, and a generous portion of porridge for breakfast, Mr. Henderland took me down to the side of the loch to visit a local fisherman. This man was crossing to the far shore to lay some nets, and he agreed to carry me, to oblige the minister. I hastily accepted the offer, as it would save me the trouble of two ferry rides around the edges of the loch. Mr. Henderland shook my hand and pressed a sixpence into my palm. I tried to refuse his gift but it was impossible, and so I left this fair-minded and kind man, waving me off from the shore.

The Linnhe Loch waters were very deep and as smooth as glass. We were so far inland, I had to taste the brine for myself before I could believe it was the salt water of the sea.

When we were halfway across, the boatman lifted his arm and pointed to a scarlet smudge on the northern shore. Every now and again I saw sparks and flashes coming from it, as though the sun was glinting off polished steel.

"Redcoats," muttered the boatman. "From Fort

William, and marching into Appin."

I remembered the last time I had seen King George's troops, and the happy pipe music and bright uniforms that had so dazzled me. The sighting of them now made me sad, as I thought of them forcefully evicting Alan's people from their farms.

As we neared the shore, I saw a channel leading into another wide body of water, and asked the boatman if this was Loch Leven. He grunted a "yes". Thanking him for his help, I clambered out into some thick woods that stretched all the way up to the rim of the valley. I found a clearing among the trees, where two pathways joined, and sat down in the bracken, to decide what to do next.

I was immediately besieged by two things: a cloud of biting flies and a terrible feeling of doubt. It occurred to me that one of these paths would lead to the south and, if I started on it today, I would reach Edinburgh in a few days. My evening with the Lowland minister had reminded me of my life in the south, my friend Mr. Campbell and the problem of my estate. On the other hand, if I journeyed on the other path, to the north, I would be siding with an outlaw who was wanted by the redcoats. But Alan was my friend, and he had risked his life to help me.

As I wrestled with this dilemma, four men emerged from one of the pathways, stepping into the clearing. They were leading their mounts behind them, as the route through the woods at this point was thin and steep.

The first man was a burly, red-haired gentleman

who fanned his florid face with a feathered hat. The second man had a black cloak and white wig and struck me as a likely member of the legal profession. The third was a servant, and he carried a great net of lemons (to brew punch with), which was a sign that the group was used to a degree of luxury. The fourth man was heavily armed, and I imagined he was in the fighting profession, perhaps a sergeant or captain.

I don't know if it was the menace of the soldier at the rear, or the sneer of the lawyer as he studied the sky, but I decided at once that I must go to my friend, Alan Breck, and offer him my services. He had saved my life on the *Covenant*, and I wanted to settle that debt. I jumped up from the bracken.

"Sir," I cried to the red-haired man, "tell me please, which path is the right one for Appin?"

The man's mouth dropped open for a second, then he turned to his lawyer. "Is this a warning, Mungo?" he bellowed. "Here we are on the road to Appin and the bracken is full of young men asking for directions to that place."

"It's no laughing matter, Colin," replied the lawyer, in a squeal of a voice. "They might know we're alone in the woods."

So this was the Red Fox, I told myself. I was glad Alan wasn't here, or his sword would be scything through the air by now.

"What do you want in Appin?" he growled.

"I'm looking for James of the Glens," I said firmly.

"You're a brave pup," he roared, "using that name around me."

"We must wait here for the soldiers," the lawyer whispered in his master's ear.

"Don't worry about me," I assured them. "I am an honest subject of King George, and not a member of the Stewart clan, or of yours."

"Why are you so far from home then?" snapped the Red Fox. "And what business do you have with the brother of the chieftain? I hold power in this country, and there are a hundred soldiers behind me, so answer truthfully."

"Are you so scared of a boy?" I joked. "I was only asking directions."

"If you'd asked me any other day but today, I would have laughed and sent a man to guide you."

"Indeed," hissed the lawyer. "It is a strange coincidence, is it not?"

I was about to assure them that I posed no threat to their party, when there was the boom of a gunshot behind me, from high in the woods. The Red Fox collapsed at my feet. "Oh, I'm shot," he cried out. The lawyer and servant tried to lift his huge body, but he only looked from one to the other with terrified, blinking eyes, and whispered, "Take care of yourselves, friends." And so he died.

The servant wailed but the lawyer stared at me in silence, with eyes hard as flints. Behind him, I could see the soldier dart back into the trees and hear him calling out to the advancing column of redcoats. I spun around and scanned the trees behind me. There was the flicker of a shape racing between them; a big man in a black cloak, carrying a long, dark shape before him.

I tore into the woods after him. "The murderer. I can see him," I called back to the lawyer. The killer was on the slope ahead of me. I dragged myself over a rock and started up the incline towards him. "He's up here," I shouted behind me.

Then I heard the icy screech of the lawyer: "Stay where you are, boy. Don't move another step."

I glanced down to the clearing which was about fifty yards below me. The redcoats were streaming in, pointing their muzzles into the trees all around them. The lawyer waved. "Come down here."

"Come up and join me," I answered. "I know which way he ran."

The lawyer snarled: "Ten pounds to the man who takes that boy. He was an accomplice, posted here in the clearing, to keep us talking so the assassin could get a clear shot."

The soldiers' rifles all turned to face me, and a wave of cold terror broke over me. I felt all the injustice of the false accusation, but I didn't want to argue against the open ends of fifty muskets.

"Duck in here with me," cried a familiar voice next to me.

I slipped behind a granite ledge and heard the guns cracking in the clearing. The thud and whine of bullets echoed around the birch trees. Alan Breck was standing next to me, clutching a fishing rod. There was no time for a warm greeting. He pulled me up the hill and we set off like two mountain goats.

We ran so fast, my heart felt as though it would burst against my ribs. Over the rocks we went, crawling through heather, dashing across the mountainside. Every few minutes, Alan would pause, and raising himself up, stare back toward the woods. Each time there was a roar and cheer from the pursuing soldiers.

At last, when I thought I could go no further, he turned to me. "Now, David of Shaws, do as I do if you value your life."

To my surprise he began picking his way back towards the woods, and soon enough we were behind the granite ledge we'd started from, panting like dogs.

My sides ached, my head swam and my tongue hung out of my mouth in a desperate thirst. We lay there, motionless, like men ready for their coffins.

Alan was the first to revive. He peered around the ledge, then came to sit by my side. "That was a tight spot, Davie, my friend. It's a good job they're too stupid to think we'd double back behind them."

I didn't respond. An hour earlier I'd seen a man in his prime, shot down in front of me, a man I knew Alan had despised. Fifty yards from the shooting, I'd found him, skulking behind a rock. It didn't make any difference to me if he'd fired the rifle, or only organized the assassination, my only friend in all that wild country was a cold-blooded murderer.

"Are you still tired?" he asked tenderly.

"No," I answered firmly, keeping my face in the bracken rather than look at him again. "We must go our separate ways, Alan. I liked you a lot, but I can't be friends with a man who can do a thing like that."

"You mean the shooting?" he asked, startled.

"Did you have no part in it?" I cried, sitting up.

"I'd never kill that man in my own country, where it will surely bring trouble on my clan. And I'd hardly be likely to bring a fishing rod along with me."

"That has a ring of truth about it," I admitted. "Do you swear it?"

He took out a dagger and held it to his heart. "I swear upon the Holy Iron, sacred to a warrior, I had no part in any of it."

I offered him my hand at once, but he seemed not to notice it.

"This is a lot of fuss over a Campbell," he huffed. "I hadn't noticed they were in short supply."

"You can't blame me for thinking you were

involved," I protested. "You were quite clear how you felt about the Red Fox, when we defended the roundhouse."

"You're right about that," said Alan with a sudden, haunted look. "I wonder if I'll come to regret my loose tongue, before this business is over. I'll be the prime suspect in the murder. But it wasn't me that fired the shot."

"Did you know the man in the black cloak?"

"I thought it was blue," he answered with a sly smile.

"Blue or black, did you know his face?"

"It's strange I confess, but I happened to be buckling my shoe when he ran past me..."

And that was all he would say about it. I knew he was trying to protect the killer, but at the same time he had exposed himself to the soldiers to rescue me, when he could have stayed hidden. Mr. Henderland's words came back to me, that we could learn a lot that was good from the wild highlanders. While I might not agree with Alan's beliefs, he was ready to die for them, and for that alone he had my respect. I put out my hand again, and this time he shook it heartily.

"We must be off," he told me. "The whole English army will be scouring Appin for us now."

"I have no fear of Scottish law," I replied proudly.

"Law?" he laughed. "You're in the Highlands now. You'd be dragged in front of a jury of fifteen Campbells, on the charge of killing a Campbell. The only justice you'd get is the same they gave to the Red Fox."

"Then I pity the legal system in your part of the country. You talk as though it's right and proper for a clan to claim a man's life, in vengeance for the death of one of their own."

"You know, Davie," he answered with a grin, "I sometimes think you Lowland farmers have no clear idea of what's right and wrong." We both laughed at this.

"If you decide to throw your lot in with me," he continued, in a more serious voice, "when I say run, you run."

"Where are you going?"

"To France, I suppose. But first I have to get down to the Lowlands. The redcoats patrol the Highland ports."

These words made me more enthusiastic about going with him. "I'll chance it with you then."

"It won't be easy," he warned me. "You'll be cold and hungry most of the time. Your life will be like a hunted deer's, and you'll sleep with your eyes half open for fear of sudden attack. It's a hard way to live, and I know it well. But that's your choice: run with me, or hang."

Some choices in life are easier than others. I eagerly put out my hand once more, and we shook on it.

We rested for an hour in the bracken before setting off to James of the Glen's house, to collect supplies to help us on our journey. Alan soon told me about the night of the shipwreck and what happened after the enormous wave that carried me into the sea.

He'd watched my driftings until he saw me gripping the floating pole. This gave him some hope that I might be washed up on the land, and was the reason for all the messages he had later left for me.

The scene he described was horrifying. As he and the sailors struggled to launch the skiff, the ship started to list and water poured into her hold. The screams from the wounded grew frantic, he told me, as they saw the water rising below them, seeping through the boards of the lower deck. At last he tumbled into the boat and a group of them rowed away, unable to save the drowning men. Two hundred yards off, another huge wave smashed into the side of the stricken *Covenant*, and she slid off the reef, onto her side. It was as though a monstrous hand was pulling her down, so steady and rapid was her descent.

During the journey to shore the men were silent, stunned by the awful screams they'd heard from the sinking ship. But, as soon as they were safe on the beach, the captain ordered his crew to grab hold of Alan. The sailors were hesitant, in no mood for more violence, but Hoseason screamed at them like a wild beast. He told them Alan's death would be their revenge for the loss of the ship and their crew-mates. It was seven against one, and they started to circle around him, drawing their knives.

It was then that Mr. Riach, perhaps suffering a sudden attack of decency, declared he couldn't watch another murder. He would stand "back to back" with the Highlander, rather than see a brave man hacked to pieces in a battle of such unfair odds.

"What happened next?" I asked Alan, anxiously.

"He told me to run, and I did. I left them arguing and brawling on the beach."

"You left Mr. Riach to face them on his own?" I cried, shocked Alan would abandon a man who was risking his life to help him.

"You have to remember, I was in Campbell country," he explained. "I'm not the most popular fellow on that coast. There were already gangs of people running toward us from the village, and I could see that the worst that would happen to Mr. Riach would be a black eye or a bloody lip. They all put their knives away as soon as I'd departed."

"Well in that case..." I said.

"As I met the Campbells on the road," he went on, chuckling, "I told them there was a wreck on the beach. When they heard there was salvage to plunder, they weren't so interested in me. I like to think it was a judgment on the Campbell clan that the ship went down in one piece, instead of breaking up. They ran all the way to the water, and didn't fish out as much as a stick."

Wanted: Dead or Alive

After three hours of quick marching through the heather, we came over the crest of a steep hill and I could see lights glittering below us. They circled and danced like fireflies, but after a few seconds I saw it was only a farmhouse with all its doors and windows open, and five or six men running around in the front yard carrying torches.

"James must be in a panic," whispered Alan. "Imagine if we were soldiers instead of friends."

He whistled a melody that rang as clear as a bell in the night air. The torches stopped moving, but when he whistled the tune once more they were immediately darting around in the same commotion as before. We hurried down the hillside and were met at the farmhouse gate by a tall, handsome man who called out to Alan in Gaelic.

"James," said Alan, "I have a friend with me, a lowlander and a laird, who never took the time to learn the language we use. Could we speak in Scots for his benefit? And, in light of the recent events, it might be better if I don't mention his name."

James of the Glens bowed and greeted me politely. When he turned back to Alan his face was lined with worry. "You've heard what's happened then? It means trouble for the clan."

"I'm not sorry to know the Fox is dead," replied Alan.

"But I wish he was alive again," answered the clan leader. "If only it had happened somewhere else. The whole of Appin will suffer now, and I have a family to think of."

The two men fell into hushed conversation about the killing, and I watched the servants bustling around the farm. Two men on a ladder were dragging guns and swords out from where they were stashed in the thatched roof above the farmhouse. The others collected the weapons and ran off into the night. Judging from the clatter of shovels and picks I could hear coming from that direction, they were burying them deep in the ground. Now and again, I caught a glimpse of their faces: white, streaked with sweat and mud, their eyes wide with fear.

As I was watching this scene, a girl stepped out of the farmhouse carrying a bundle of clothes. Alan glanced over at her, and broke off his discussion. "What's she got there?" he asked suspiciously.

James shook his head. "Do you think I could keep French clothes in my house, with a hundred redcoats about to storm down the valley and search it. All the guns are being buried and the clothes go in with them."

"Bury my clothes?" Alan cried. "In the mud? I don't think so." And he snatched the parcel from the girl's hands and retreated to the barn to change.

When he returned, he looked more like his old self in his fine French outfit.

I was given fresh clothes myself, and a pair of shoes made out of deerskin. Our other supplies for the journey were a sword and pistol each, a bag of porridge oats, a saucepan and a bottle of good French brandy. Alan was satisfied that we had everything we needed to be "out on the heather", but his mouth dropped open when James told him how much money he could give us. It was only a few shillings.

"Davie, what's left in your purse?" Alan asked me.

"Not much more than two pounds," I answered.

"It's not enough," he cried. "James, you'll have to find more."

"I can't, Alan. You'll have to reach a safe place, then send a message back to me. In a few days I'll be able to raise some cash for you."

"I'll be relying on that, James," Alan whispered but I could see he was uneasy about this plan.

We said our farewells, and stepped out into the mild, dark night, with a long journey ahead of us.

Sometimes we walked, sometimes we ran; and as the night sky grew lighter we ran more and walked less. We had to find shelter before the bright light of the day made it even more dangerous to travel.

But by the time the sun was almost full in the sky we were still out in the open, crossing a wide valley. It was strewn with great granite boulders and a river in full flood cut through the middle of it. There were no trees or thick bushes to hide in, and I could see that Alan was worried.

He sprinted down to the waterside, where the river was split into rapids by three flat rocks. It was so loud it made my stomach tremble and there was a mist of spray hanging in the air.

Alan didn't hesitate. I watched him launch himself from the rock at the edge and land on all fours, on the middle stone. Without thinking of the risks I followed him, and he caught me before I tumbled into the flood.

We stood next to each other, staring at the far bank. It was a much longer jump than the first. I looked around at the wide river and the wet rocks and felt my arms and legs trembling with fear. Alan grabbed my shoulders and shook me. I could see his mouth shouting in my face, but the river was so thunderous it was impossible to hear. I felt my legs go numb and covered my ears to try to block out the sound of the water. My heart was racing and I felt dizzy. Alan lifted the brandy to my lips and forced me to drink. The sting of the alcohol brought the blood back and I began to breathe more easily. He put his hands to his mouth, and then cupped them to my ear. "Hang or drown," he screamed. Then he turned his back on me, leapt, and landed safely on the far shore.

I knew that if I didn't do it at once, I would never do it at all. I bent my knees and threw myself forward. My hands caught the river bank, slipped, caught again, but my body was sliding back into the rapids. Alan seized me by the hair, then the collar, and hauled me in like a caught fish.

He didn't speak. He started running, and I ran after him. I was tired, sick and bruised, and a little drunk. I felt a stitch burning in my side, but I ran until he stopped under two enormous rocks, leaning against each other.

I watched as he scrambled up the rock face. When he reached the summit he let down a rope, and with my last scrap of strength I pulled myself up.

Then I saw why he had wanted to reach this spot. The two rocks were both worn away at the top, and they formed a hollow crater, about twenty feet from the ground, big enough for three men to lie hidden.

Only when he had scanned the entire valley did he turn back to me with a smile. "You're not much of a rock-jumper are you?" he chuckled.

I was too weary to speak, but he must have guessed I wasn't pleased.

"But that's a sign of true bravery," he said quickly,

"to do something even when you're scared of it. And water's a horrible thing, though it does have its uses. For that, I owe you an apology?"

"What are you talking about?"

"I forgot to ask James for a water bottle. You may think that's not important, but it could be a long, hot day ahead of us."

I licked my lips and found they were dry as paper. "Empty out the brandy bottle," I panted, "and I'll run back to the river and fill it up."

"The brandy was useful," he laughed. "It might be useful again. And you might have noticed I was running quite quickly up from the river."

"I noticed," I said, rubbing my aching legs.

"There was a reason for that," he smiled. "You'll find out in good time. For now, I suggest you get some sleep, while I keep watch."

I didn't argue. We'd been on the move for six hours and I was dog-tired. Soon I was snoozing on a bed of soft bracken.

I woke with Alan's hand pressing down on my mouth.

"Silence," he whispered. "You were snoring." And he pointed toward the edge of the rock basin. I peered over.

It was now a cloudless, dazzling day and though I guessed it was no more than nine o'clock, the air was already sultry. Half a mile along the river, there was a camp of redcoats, with hundreds of them gathered around a blazing fire: cooking, erecting tents and

checking their equipment. On a rock next to the camp, almost as high as ours, I could see a guard standing to attention, his rifle sparkling in the sun. All along the river there were other guards, some alone, some marching in pairs. And, further up the river, where the ground was less rocky, there was a detachment of dragoons, with their horses grazing around the tents. What had been a bare plain of rocks and river, was now a small town of redcoats.

"They started coming in about an hour ago," whispered Alan, "singing as they marched. Davie, you could sleep through a hurricane," he added with a smile. "I thought they might station a command post here to stop us from getting through. That's why I was in a hurry to reach this rock. We'll try slipping past them tonight."

"What do we do till then?" I asked him, my heart pounding.

"Lie here and scorch."

As he predicted, we lay on that rock like steaks on a griddle. The heat grew ever fiercer as the afternoon wore on. We didn't have a drop of water, and the brandy only made our thirst worse. Lying there sweating, I listened to the soldiers scouting around the rocks. Sometimes they came so close to our hideout, we were scared to breathe in case they heard us.

At two o'clock the sun was so hot I thought I could smell my hair sizzling on the stone. Alan suddenly tapped me on the arm, and we both climbed down to the ground, as quietly as we could manage.

"Could you try running again?" Alan hissed in my ear.

"Anything but return to that stove," I answered. "I'd rather face a bayonet than climb up there again."

We began to slip from one rock to the next, staying in the shade, crawling on our bellies. At dusk we were almost at the edge of the valley, and here we came across an icy stream gushing down to the river. We plunged our heads and shoulders in. I've never been so grateful for the taste of water.

We mixed our porridge oats with the water and made a simple meal, and after the sunset we started picking our way along a steep path that led us out of the valley. After an hour of stealthy climbing, we were up on the ridge of a mountain, and Alan paused to check his direction. The night had brought a string of clouds with it, and they were stretched out to one side of us, lit by the moon. Ahead of us loomed the black heads of mountains, and down below I could see the glimmer of the stars, reflected on a mighty sea loch.

"We're safe now," Alan chuckled. And then, knowing we were out of earshot of the redcoats, he started whistling a jaunty Highland tune, that made my feet step faster.

Before that night was over we came down to a cleft in the mountains. Hidden behind a wood of birch trees, at the base of the mountain, was a shallow cave. This cave was to be our home for the next five days and nights.

There was a small lake full of trout in the heart of the woods and cuckoos and doves fluttered around in the trees. We were able to make a small fire in the cave, without fearing the smoke would be detected. Here we ate hot porridge and grilled the little trout we caught in the lake.

This idyllic spot was the "safe place" from which Alan intended to send a message to James.

"But how will you send a note?" I joked with him. "Will you train a cuckoo to carry one for you?"

"Oh Davie," he sighed, "you lowlanders have no ingenuity."

After staring into the fire for ten minutes, deep in thought, he went off and fetched a piece of wood. He cut it and fastened it across the middle to make a cross. "May I have the button I gave you, Davie?" he asked. "It will only be a temporary loan."

He tied the button to one arm of the cross. Then he took a piece of birch bark and a fishbone and fixed these to two other arms. "There is a hamlet a few miles from here," he told me. "I've got friends there, Davie, that I'd trust with my life. But there are others living there whom I'm not so sure of. By now there'll be a reward on our heads. And gold and silver can make a person weak... and talkative."

"So what will you do?"

"I'll creep down there tonight, under cover of dark, and leave this sign I've made in the window of Mr. John Maccoll, a loyal friend of mine."

"I don't see how that will help us," I replied.

"Well, John isn't a genius, but I hope he will see the sign and understand its message. The wooden cross is the rallying symbol for our clan, to call members together when the clan is in trouble. But he will know the clan isn't gathering because there is no note with the cross to tell him where to go. Then he will see the button, and he will know that it belonged

117

to my father, and he will think of me. With any luck he'll put the two ideas together and realize that Duncan's son is in trouble and needs him to go to him."

"I'm impressed so far, Alan," I admitted. "But how will he know where you are?"

"John will see the birch and think to himself, *Alan is in a birch wood.*"

"And the fishbone will tell him the woods are next to a lake?"

"I hope so," replied Alan laughing. "And if he's too stupid to work it out, he isn't worth the salt in his porridge."

"It is a brilliant plan," I said to him, with a hint of mockery, "but a lowlander would leave him a hand-written note."

"Not so ingenious," replied Alan, "when you consider that John would have to go to school for three or four years to learn how to read it. We might get tired of waiting for him."

That night Alan left the cross in his friend's window. The next day we lay hidden at the edge of the woods, keeping a careful vigil, and at noon we saw a solitary man approaching through the heather. Alan whistled to him, and he soon joined us by the fireside in our cave.

He was a ragged, bearded man, poorly dressed and grossly disfigured by smallpox. Our first problem was that he refused to take a message to James unless it was in the form of a letter. He was worried James might think he was a liar if he just turned up at his house with a story about Alan needing money. It had to be a letter, or he wouldn't go at all.

I witnessed Alan's resourcefulness once more with his construction of the tools and materials necessary for letter-writing. He found the body of a dove and from its wing he plucked a quill. For ink he mixed the black gunpowder from his pistol with water from the stream. For paper he tore off a corner from his French military commission (which he always carried with him, perhaps thinking it would give him diplomatic immunity from the gallows). I watched him write:

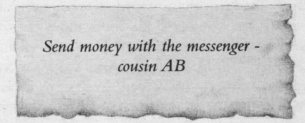

*Send money with the messenger -
cousin AB*

John Maccoll took the note, stuffed it deep inside his scruffy trousers and promised to be back as quickly as possible.

Three days later we heard him whistling at the edge of the woods. He sat down by the fire, warmed his hands and gave us the news from around the country. It was alive with redcoats and they were searching every house and farm for the fugitives; James had been thrown in prison under suspicion of complicity in the murder; and there were whispers everywhere that it was Alan Breck who had done the deed. A reward of one hundred pounds was offered for our capture.

"Is there a wanted poster, John?" Alan asked anxiously.

"There is," the man replied, with a hint of a smile. "It's a good description of you, Alan, and your fancy clothes. Though it describes them as 'tarnished with wear' I'm afraid."

"Tarnished?" cried Alan. "Those redcoat dogs insult me. What about the lowlander?"

"The details they give could fit any boy his age."

When I heard these words I remembered my feelings in the woods by the loch. If I were to take another path home, away from Alan (and his telltale clothes), it was unlikely that anyone would recognize me from the description given on the poster. Even if I were arrested, there would be nothing to prove that I'd been involved in the crime. But, if I were arrested with Alan, the prime suspect, it would be assumed I was his accomplice. I felt ashamed to be thinking of saving my own skin. But, after all, the hatred between the Highland clans was none of my business.

James' wife had only sent us five pounds. This made me even more tempted to go my own way. Alan had to reach France with this money, and I was only going as far as Edinburgh.

"It's not as much as I was hoping for," he said, staring over at me, "but it should see us both out of danger."

My sense of guilt intensified when I heard him say this. I was thinking I'd be better off away from him, while he was convinced he was serving, helping and protecting me. I bit my lip and told myself I must take my chances with this brave man.

Our messenger went back in the direction of his cozy cottage, with its fire and bed, while we started tramping in the direction of a distant mountain range, moving away from all human comforts.

The Chase
on the Moor

After twelve hours of hiking, we stopped in a ditch, at the edge of a wide, flat moor. The sun had been up for an hour, and it shone straight in our eyes, and a thin mist hung a few feet above the rolling ground.

"There could be a thousand dragoons hidden out there," whispered Alan, "and we'd be none the wiser."

"Do we have to cross it?"

"Appin is behind us to the west," he explained. "To the south lies the land of the Campbells, and to the north there are the redcoat forts. You want to get home and I need to rent a boat. My hope was to strike east towards Queensferry, but I'd forgotten about this desert of open moorland."

"Can we rest here and cross at night?" I asked him.

"The mountains aren't far behind us," he answered. "Any redcoat with a telescope could see us if he was perched up there. We need to keep moving until we find cover."

"East it is then," I said as cheerfully as I could manage. But at the same moment I was thinking: *Let us take opposite points of the compass and it would be the best for both of us.*

Alan slapped me on the shoulder. "Good lad," he whispered. "But it's a dangerous crossing. If we're spotted by a mounted patrol, they could ride us down like hounds hunting rabbits. Our swords would be no match for theirs. And the lance is a dreadful weapon."

"I give you my word, Alan," I whispered, determined not to betray him, despite my doubts, "I'll keep moving until we drop."

His eyes flickered with pride and he shook my hand. "There are times when you're too much of a King George's man for my liking. And other times when I love you like a brother."

The moor was as flat and desolate as the sea. The only sound was the skitter of moorhens in the scrub and the cry of a hawk, circling in the sky. It was the most deserted place I had ever seen, but at least it was empty of our hunters, the English troops.

We began creeping through the heather. At noon we stopped to rest, and Alan took the first watch. I had just closed my eyes when he was shaking me by the shoulder.

"Have you seen something?" I asked him.

"No. But you've been asleep three hours and now it's my turn."

I could hardly believe that more than a few minutes had passed. As I was rubbing my eyes, he stuck a sprig of heather in the ground to act as a sun clock. "When the shadow falls over to the East," he whispered, marking the spot with a line in the soil, "you can wake me."

But I had never really woken from my own sleep. My limbs were so heavy with fatigue, I couldn't lift a hand to my face. The heather was hot and soft like a cotton quilt, and the drone of the bees was a lullaby in my ears. Every now and again I would give a little shudder and know that I had been fast asleep.

The last time this happened I looked down at the sprig of heather and my heart missed a beat. The shadow was well past the point that Alan had marked. I'd been asleep for hours.

I'd betrayed Alan's trust. I felt a wave of shame well up in me, but what I saw next made my blood cold with fear. A line of cavalry was approaching from the south, shoving their long, steel lances into every clump of heather to make sure there was no one hiding there.

When I woke Alan he looked at the mark in the soil, then at the redcoats and then across at me. There was no need for him to say anything in reproach. I could see everything from his expression. His disappointment in me doubled my own feeling of shame.

"Now we play at being the rabbits," he muttered. He pointed to the northeast, to a range of black hills. "That's a thick forest. If we can get there by morning, we'll live another day."

"But that takes us across the path of the soldiers," I whispered.

"There's no going back, Davie," he replied. "Remember what you promised."

We started scuttling forward through the heather, down on our hands and knees. This brought up a fine dust that choked and blinded me, and soon my wrists and ankles were aching, as though they were being squeezed by steel bands. Every time we came to a dip or found enough heather to shelter us, we paused to catch our breath. The dragoons were advancing, beating the undergrowth as they came, and I could see that we were slowly slipping to the eastern side of them.

After another hour I was ready to drop and die of exhaustion. It was only the fear of what Alan would say if I failed him again that kept me moving. My throat was dry as sand with the dust, my muscles were knotted and cramping and my head pounded in pain.

There was the sudden blast of a trumpet sounding

behind us, and we crashed down, peering over the heather to see what was happening. The dragoons were making camp.

"Alan," I begged, "can we rest now? They've stopped, haven't they?"

"There shall be no sleep for us tonight," he snapped back at me.

"I can't go on," I confessed. "I'll die if I take another step."

"Then I'll carry you," he answered.

Once again I felt a wave of shame. "Lead on, and I'll follow," I muttered.

Night fell as we scampered for the edge of the moor. The air grew cooler, bringing a light rain, which refreshed my energies a little. But I was still so tired that I hardly knew who or where I was. All I could think of was the next step, the next clump of heather to crawl over, the next rock to avoid crashing into.

When daylight came, Alan said it was safe to run standing up, and at last I could get up from the ground, instead of crawling like an animal. We were so tired we ran along, doubled-over like old men with bad backs. We stared down at our shuffling feet, concentrating all our energy into the effort of lifting them.

Finally, at the eastern edge of the moor, Alan flopped down into the heather and whispered: "We're safe." I lay next to him, my whole body pulsing with agony.

"Now we can sleep for an hour or two," he muttered, and within seconds I could hear him snoring.

But I was too racked with aches and cramped muscles to be able to rest. I had felt a dreadful heaviness out on the moor, but now that was replaced with an awful feeling of lightness. I imagined my body turning into the same powdery dust we'd been breathing in our flight.

Then we were marching again. We marched on and on, until we were lost in a labyrinth of dreary valleys and craggy hollows and the sun vanished in the sky.

The next day, the weather grew colder, and I weaker. I felt as though we had been walking for a thousand years. There were times I thought I would lie down and die in the heather, like an old sheep or fox, and leave my bones to whiten in the Highlands.

"Alan, if you don't help me," I cried suddenly, "I'll die here. Take me to a house, and let me die."

"Can you walk?" he asked softly, crossing to my side. "Here, lean on me."

"When I'm dead, Alan," I sobbed, "please try to forgive me for failing you."

"Come on," he replied tenderly, "I'll find us a house, though I can't tell you who will open the door. It could be anyone: redcoat, Campbell, friend or foe."

A Pipe Contest

We were lucky and chanced upon the household of a friendly clan, the Maclarens. Alan's reputation with them was enough to earn me good treatment for the course of my illness – a whole three weeks. They fetched me a doctor and tended to me as though I was a relative.

By day, Alan hid in the woods, just outside the village, and at night he crept into the village to join me. The owner of the house, Duncan, was a music lover, and owned a set of Highland pipes. After dinner, he and Alan would pull two chairs over to my bedside, and take turns playing tunes for me.

The time passed without incident, except for one evening when I had a visit from a mysterious gentleman. He was the son of that Scottish rogue and outlaw, Rob Roy, and his name was Robin. He was an enemy of the Maclaren clan but he walked into Duncan's house as coolly as if he had stopped for a drink at a local tavern.

"I've been told," he began, towering over me, "that your name is Balfour."

"David Balfour," I said softly, "at your service."

"My family owes your family a good deed," he

went on. "My brother's leg was smashed in battle, and the surgeon that saved it shared your name. I want to repay the debt. Ask me anything, and I will make sure it is done."

But I knew nothing about the history of the Shaws. I had to admit to Robin (in bitter disgrace) that I knew little about my illustrious ancestors. He sneered at me, for in the Highlands they think a man is worthless if he doesn't know his past, then left my bedside without another word.

As he stepped to the door, he met Alan coming into the room.

The two, proud warriors backed away from each other and their hands settled on the hilts of their swords. Neither of them were tall men, but they seemed to swell and grow with their pride, like peacocks fanning their tails.

"Alan Breck," said Robin boldly. "I didn't know you were in my country."

"And here was I," replied Alan in a firm voice, "thinking this was the country of my friends, the Maclarens."

"We could debate that," Robin said with a scowl, "or we could settle the question with our swords."

"Any time you're ready," cried Alan, taking another step back and preparing to draw his sword.

"Gentlemen," interrupted Duncan. "This is my house and I've another challenge in mind than swords. I've heard that you're both skilled pipers. It's an old argument in the Maclaren clan, to see which of you is the best musician, and tonight we can settle the dispute."

"Is it true that you're a piper?" muttered Alan to Robin.

"I can pipe the birds out of the trees," Robin answered.

"That's fighting talk," replied Alan.

"I've made bolder talk, and beaten better adversaries. Fetch your pipes, old man."

Duncan returned with his pipes, a side of ham and a bottle of whisky. The two rival clan members sat down, on either side of a glowing peat fire. They took a bite of ham and a cup of whisky and then they got ready to play.

Robin went first, playing a simple tune with no flourishes.

"Is that the best you can do?" cried Alan confidently, reaching for the pipes. Then he repeated the same tune, adding new notes and changing the rhythm so it sounded fresh to my ears. It was an impressive performance. Alan was in the lead.

"Hand them back," whispered Robin. He started the tune again, and this time I had never heard such sweet playing. Alan's face grew dark with jealousy. Finally he could take no more and he shouted, "Enough. You're a fine piper. Be glad we chose this contest and not the swords."

Then Robin began playing a tune that was a traditional melody of the Appin Stewarts. Alan's expression softened at once. By the end of the piece, all signs of his anger in defeat had died away.

"Robin," he said humbly, "you are a great piper, the greatest I have ever heard. Of course, when it comes to swords it could be different, but on the pipes, you're the master. You have more music in your little fingers than I do in my whole body."

After this the whisky started flowing and I watched the three men laughing and playing the pipes until the morning sun was high in the sky.

To Queensferry Town

After thanking the Maclarens for their kindness, we walked fifteen miles to the house of a good friend of Duncan's. We left there at midnight, and the next day found us snuggled up in a heather bush, basking in the sunshine and snoozing until dusk.

At dawn we arrived at the River Forth, and as we followed it down to the vast plain of Stirling, Alan tapped me on my arm. "We're back in your country now, Davie," he told me. "We've crossed into the Lowlands."

I was so elated to be back in my homeland, I suggested to Alan that we could march straight across the bridge at Stirling and follow the road all the way to Queensferry.

"And I suppose the redcoats would shake our hands and lend us a carriage to ride in as well," he joked. "We're not out of the woods yet, Davie. We must cross the Forth in stealth, and find your lawyer friend..."

"Mr. Rankeillor?" I cried.

"And hope he can raise some money for us. You haven't forgotten that the greater part of my voyage lies ahead of me, Davie, have you?"

"I'll do what I can to help you find a ship, Alan, I promise."

He shook my hand and thanked me. "Then the safest route would be to follow the river east and find a boat to take us across. It's too wide to be swum and all the bridges are watched by guards."

"How can we rent a boat?" I asked him, "with an empty purse." Nearly all our money was paid to my doctor.

"Ingenuity," he chuckled. And I followed after him along the riverbank.

By morning, hungry and foot-sore, we were on the outskirts of the hamlet of Limekilns. The smoke was rising from the chimneys of Queensferry on the opposite shore. I thought of my inheritance and wealth waiting for me on the other side of the river, and me standing here in torn and filthy clothes, only five shillings in my purse and with a price on my head.

We found a tavern and used the last of our money to buy some bread and cheese, then retired to some nearby woods to make sandwiches and stare across the water at the last, watery mile of our journey, that was causing us so much difficulty.

"Did you notice the pretty girl who sold us our lunch?" asked Alan suddenly.

"This is not the time to be talking about pretty girls," I replied curtly.

"Well, I noticed that she had a good look at you, a good, long look. It's a shame you're not as pale as you were a week ago," he continued, "but you still have a hounded, death's-door expression on your face. I think, Davie, I have a plan."

And before I could ask him what he was talking about, he had left me there in the woods, ordering me to stay hidden until I heard his call.

It was past eleven o'clock at night when I heard the soft whistle of my friend. I popped my head over the long grass by the river and saw him bobbing in a small boat, scanning the shore for me. The girl from the tavern held the ores at the stern.

I waded out to the boat, and was about to say my thanks to her when Alan put his hand over my mouth. "Not a word," he whispered in my ear. "The sound carries on the water."

So we rowed in silence, and when we reached the other shore, she shook our hands and was out again on the river before I had a chance to thank her. I turned to Alan: "But why did she help us?" I asked in amazement.

"She heard a moving story," said Alan with a smile.

"About a good prince, kidnapped by evil men, and how he fought his way back to the Lowlands against all dangers, to reclaim his kingdom."

"You told her that?" I said in disbelief.

"It was not so far from the truth, was it? And now," he went on before I could answer, "we have an appointment with a certain lawyer in the morning. Let's get some rest."

We slept in a copse by the road that led into Queensferry, and at dawn I left Alan hiding there, arranging to meet him at dusk.

Queensferry was an elegant market town and I felt as badly dressed as a scarecrow walking past its fine shops and well-dressed inhabitants. I was so nervous about the impending meeting with the lawyer, I decided to walk around the town until my nerves had calmed. After an hour of traipsing around, I found myself standing before a fine mansion house. A dog was yawning on the porch step, and he looked so at home there, I was envious of him.

As I studied the sleepy guard-dog, the front door of the house swung open and a man with a sharp face and bright eyes, in a white wig and spectacles, stepped out onto the porch. He looked at me, a lonely urchin in rags, and he asked me politely if he could be of any assistance.

"I am here on business, sir," I replied. "Could you please direct me to the house of Mr. Rankeillor?"

"You are here, at his house," he said briskly. "And I am he."

"Then I must beg an interview," I asked awkwardly.

He led me past the dozy hound and into his house, to a dusty little room full of books and documents. "Please be seated," he said, glancing from his fine leather chair to the muddy rags I wore. "Be brief and to the point," he added, adjusting his spectacles.

"My name is David Balfour," I said as boldly as I could manage, "and I am the true laird of the estate of Shaws."

"Really," he replied, twirling a pen between his long, slender fingers. "Have you any papers to prove this wild claim, Mr. Balfour?"

"Not with me," I muttered.

"I see."

"But there are some in the hands of Mr. Campbell of Essendean, and he would swear to my identity. I do not believe my uncle could deny it either."

"You mean, Ebenezer Balfour, I assume?"

I nodded my head.

"Have you ever come across a man named Hoseason?" he asked suddenly. I jumped up from my chair.

"Yes, sir, he was an agent of my uncle in their plan to sell me as a slave..."

"A slave?" said the lawyer in a mocking tone.

"They kidnapped me and threatened me with slavery. But there was a shipwreck..."

"Where was this shipwreck?" he asked, in the same

doubting voice.

"Off the Isle of Mull," I replied.

"That part of your story, at least, matches other facts I have at my disposal. But what do you mean by saying you were kidnapped?"

"I was knocked unconscious and thrown into the hold, sir."

"I see," he said with a thin smile. "I know the ship was lost on the 27th of June," and he turned the pages of a document on his desk as he told me this. "It is now August the 24th. What have you been doing for two months, Mr. Balfour?"

"Before I go on, sir," I said meekly, "I would like to know if I am talking to a friend."

"How can I tell you that," he asked angrily, "before I know all the facts?"

"I was kidnapped on the orders of my own uncle, and while I have no doubts concerning your honesty, sir, I know that he was your employer."

Mr. Rankeillor laughed out loud at this remark. "I've done some work for him in the past," he admitted, "but while you've been gone, a lot of water has run under the bridge."

"How do you mean, sir?" I asked.

"Well," he began, leaning back in his chair, "on the day your ship was sinking into the waves, the good minister of Essendean stormed into this office and demanded to know what had happened to a certain David Balfour. I am a magistrate in this town and one of my responsibilities is to receive any reports of missing persons. Mr. Campbell said that you were missing. He had been waiting for a message, or a visit from you, and thought it was unlike you to forget your loyalty to a friend. I didn't know of your existence until that day, but I did know your father, and as soon as I heard that he had a son, I feared the worst.

"I set off to see Ebenezer and, under interrogation, he claimed he had given you a large sum of money and sent you off to Europe. He told me you wanted to start a new life on the continent."

"The scoundrel," I cried out, unable to restrain myself any longer.

"I did have my suspicions," the lawyer said softly, "but then Mr. Hoseason reported your death by drowning. Our case against Ebenezer was lost. Mr. Campbell is heartbroken, I have lost my client and, as no one believed your uncle was telling the truth, the reputation of his character has grown even worse, if such a thing is possible."

"But I am alive, sir," I shouted.

"So I see. And if you trust me now, after hearing my story, I would be most interested in hearing yours."

He closed his eyes and drummed his fingers on the table as I told him of my adventures. Twenty minutes had passed and his face was so still I thought he might be snoozing, but when I mentioned the name Alan Breck he sat up in his chair and held a hand in the air.

"No unnecessary names please, Mr. Balfour. This is not the time to bring up Highland politics."

"As you wish, sir, but as I've mentioned it now, I may as well continue to use it."

"Perhaps I should have told you at the start of our interview, Mr. Balfour, that I am an old man and my hearing can be unreliable. I believe you used the name Mr. Thomson, didn't you? Please continue to use that name, and to use it for any other Highland characters you encountered in your travels – dead or alive."

I realized he must have guessed that I had some knowledge of the murder of the Red Fox, and was anxious to avoid hearing anything that might endanger me or himself. For the rest of my story I used Mr. Thomson to mean Alan, and called the other highlanders I had met, Mr. Thomson the second, Mr. Thomson the third, and so on.

When I had finished, Mr. Rankeillor congratulated me. "You have been on an epic journey, my lad. You've rambled across half of Scotland by the sound of it. But I think now you are near to the end of your troubles. We must, of course, resolve the dual issues of Mr. Thomson's safe onward voyage, and the return of your estate. I will help in any way I can. I propose to start by offering you a bowl of hot water, some soap and a suit from my son's wardrobe."

Without another word, he escorted me up the staircase to one of the bedrooms, and left me alone to get changed.

The Beggar Returns

It was a relief to look in a mirror on the wall and see the David Balfour I remembered. I'd been knocked about and ravaged with illness, but the experience hadn't left me with too many scars, and my skin looked healthy and tanned from being out in the elements.

Mr. Rankeillor knocked on my door after an hour and asked me to join him again in his study.

"I want to tell you a story," he began, as soon as we were seated, "about your father and your uncle. It starts with a love affair."

"My uncle was in love?" I cried.

"He was young and handsome once, Davie. He had a fine, gallant air, and people came out to wave hello to him whenever he rode by upon his stallion."

"I can hardly believe it," I stammered.

"The brothers fell in love with the same girl. And Ebenezer, who was always used to getting his own way, was the loser. I've never seen a man fall into disgrace so quickly. He began drinking heavily, spent weeks in bed trying to milk sympathy from his family, and told your father he would die of a broken heart. After months of suffering the wrath of his spoiled and selfish brother, your decent father decided to offer him the estate, while he would marry the lady.

"It was foolish generosity on your father's part. I suppose he wanted a quiet life, and the love of your mother was more than enough compensation for renouncing his wealth. But look at the trouble his good deed has caused us all.

"Ebenezer was left with nothing to value but gold, and so he grew miserly and grasping. Whispers started about the sudden disappearance of your father and soon people were saying Ebenezer had murdered him and taken the Hall by violence."

"But where does this leave me?" I asked him. "Is the Shaws mine?"

"Without question, you are the rightful laird. But Ebenezer will fight the ruling of the court, and family law cases can take years to resolve."

"That's not encouraging news," I sighed.

"There's worse to come," he went on. "If he hears anything of your involvement with Mr. Thomson, he could use it to stain your character in the eyes of the jury."

"Then what should I do?" I cried, despairingly.

"Let Ebenezer remain in the Hall until his natural death. In the meantime he can give you a fair share of the income from the estate. You'll still be a rich man. Of course," he added, "getting money out of a miser of Ebenezer's proportions will test our ingenuity to its limits."

"Ingenuity?" I cried. There was a plan forming in

my mind. "I know a man who can help us with that."

"Not your Mr. Thomson?" the lawyer groaned.

"He's the most ingenious man in Scotland."

"And the most wanted," he replied. "But what is your plan?"

"We must use Ebenezer's involvement in the crime of my kidnapping to our advantage," I told him excitedly.

"A cunning idea," whispered Mr. Rankeillor, nodding his head. "But it would be hard to prove in court. We must surprise him."

He got up from his desk and called for his servant. When the man came in, Rankeillor scribbled down a note and passed it to him. "Draw up a legal contract with these facts. And be ready to join us in an hour. You might be needed as a witness." The man bowed and left the room.

"So you're willing to try my plan?" I asked him.

"Of course," he smiled. "There's just time for me to enjoy a glass of wine, while you explain the details."

We set off, the three of us, on the road out of town and towards the woods where Alan lay in hiding. At one point in the walk, we passed the Hawes Inn. The landlord was sitting in the garden, smoking a pipe, and I was stunned to see that he didn't look a day older than I remembered. Only two months had passed, but I felt wiser by years, when I thought of myself, wide-eyed and excited, staring out at the sailing ship.

At the edge of the woods, Mr. Rankeillor fell back with his man-servant and I went ahead, whistling for Alan. He popped out from behind a tree and hugged me.

"Look at you," he cried, "dressed as though we're going to a dance." I quickly told him my plan. "It's well-conceived," he complimented me. "But it will take a smooth-talker to accomplish it, a gentleman of great intelligence. Myself, for example."

"It was you I had in mind," I replied.

"But what about the lawyer?" whispered Alan, suddenly concerned. "He won't want to be seen in my company, Davie. It would place him in danger with the redcoats."

Just then I heard Mr. Rankeillor calling out behind me on the road: "Davie," he cried with a sly grin, "you haven't seen my glasses anywhere, have you? I must have dropped them. Without my glasses, I can't recognize my own mother. Who is that you are talking with?"

He crossed the grass and came over to us. Alan put out his hand and the two men greeted one another politely.

"You must be Mr. Thomson," said the lawyer in a soft voice, and Alan understood his scheme at once. "Forgive me, Mr. Thomson," added Rankeillor, "if I pass you on the road tomorrow and fail to identify you. Without my glasses, I see nothing and nobody. Now, shouldn't we be on our way?"

It was after ten when we reached the House of Shaws. As I'd expected, there were no lights burning in the windows. After stopping for a last consultation, a hundred yards away in the darkness, we three witnesses took our positions hiding in the grass, while Alan strode over to the nail-studded door, and began to knock.

After a moment we heard the scrape of a musket on the windowsill, and the familiar whine of my uncle's voice. "Who are you, and what do you want?"

"It's about David," replied Alan.

In the still, night air I could almost hear my uncle gulping in shock. "You'd better come in," he said after a pause, in a sinister voice.

"No," replied Alan firmly. "I'm taking no chances inside your house. Come down to the porch to talk."

There was silence for a whole minute, and I worried that my uncle wouldn't take the bait. But at last he slipped out of the door, the rifle pointing straight at Alan's chest. "What's your business," he growled.

"If you are a gentleman blessed with any insight," Alan began, "you will have realized from my accent that I've journeyed from the Highlands. My name is unimportant but my people come from the Isle of Mull."

Even in the gloom of the summer night I could see Ebenezer's face twitching and contorting with fear.

"I see you have heard of the place," said Alan. "Perhaps you also heard there was a shipwreck there, not long ago. The morning after the disaster, one of

my clan was out searching for firewood on the beach, when he came across a boy, half-drowned, but still breathing. He was taken to an old ruined castle and thrown in a cell, and there he's been living for two months, at great expense to my poor relations.

"My clansmen are poor, Mr. Balfour, and life's a hard business on Mull. I've been sent here to negotiate for the ransom money, and if it's not paid promptly, you'll never see the lad again."

"You can do what you want with the boy," Ebenezer spat. "He was never much use to me."

Alan smiled at him and winked, "You're a cunning old fox, Mr. Balfour. You think by pretending not to care, I'll agree to a lower ransom payment?"

"I always mean what I say," answered my uncle viciously. "I don't care what you do with him."

And now Alan's acting ability was tested to its limits. He was so convincing I almost believed I was a prisoner in the Highlands, and not hiding by the wall of the house, ten feet away. "You can't be serious?" he cried. "Think of the shame of deserting your own nephew, and what the townsfolk would say if they found out about it."

"They wouldn't say anything," said Ebenezer with a sneer, "because I wouldn't tell them. And neither would you or your criminal family, for fear of the law."

"Then David will have to tell them," said Alan.

"What do you mean?" shrieked my uncle.

"My family won't keep him if there's no money in it. We'll have to let him go."

"You can't do that."

"I can't pretend to understand you lowlanders," said Alan. "I thought you'd be glad we were letting him go. Now I wonder if you'd rather we killed the boy."

"It's a possibility, isn't it?" muttered Ebenezer.

"What a strange man you are?" cried Alan. "Do you want us to keep him in the castle, or kill him? Either way we'll expect to be paid, and I can't say I mind which it is. So tell me, kill him, or keep him?"

It took a moment for my uncle to decide. "Keep him," he whispered, with a disappointed look in his eye.

"That's the more expensive option," said Alan.

"I was worried you'd say that," replied Ebenezer. "But I don't want any more bloodshed. After all, he's my brother's son."

"Fair enough," answered Alan. "Now, what about the fee? If you tell me what you paid Hoseason, I'll be able to fix a proper price with you."

"Hoseason?" cried my uncle. "What's he got to do with it?"

"The kidnapping of course," said Alan, looking perplexed. "We know all about it from David."

"It's a lie," screamed my uncle.

"You don't think I'm a fool, do you, Mr. Balfour?" said Alan softly. "I've spoken with Hoseason; we're partners in this. If you ask me, you never should have trusted that old sailor with your private business, but what's done is done, so there's no point acting so innocent now."

"Did he tell you what I gave him?" demanded my uncle.

"To answer that would weaken my bargaining position, Mr. Balfour."

"Well he's a liar," spat my uncle. "I swear on my life I only gave him twenty pounds for the kidnapping. On top of that he was to get the money from the slave merchants. But I only paid twenty."

"Thank you, Mr. Thomson," said the lawyer,

jumping up from the grass. "We have everything we need now. Good evening, Mr. Balfour."

"Good evening, *uncle*," I cried, leaping up.

"Good, evening, sir," added the servant.

Ebenezer sat on the step of the door like a man turned to stone. We picked him up under the arms and carried him into the kitchen.

"Fetch the best bottle of wine from the cellar," cried Mr. Rankeillor. "We should have a celebration."

When we all had a full glass in our hand (except Ebenezer) the lawyer asked my uncle to join him in the library, to sign the contract he had drawn up. When they came out again, I was entitled to two-thirds of the annual income from the estate. Ebenezer gave me a limp handshake, and retired to his room, where we locked him in for the night.

So the beggar in the old folk song had claimed his rightful inheritance. After sixty days of making my bed on heather, dirt and stones, hungry and in fear of death, I passed my first sleepless night, there in the House of Shaws. I was awake until dawn, busy making plans for the future.

The Parting Time

At last I was safe and had found my rightful place in life, but my best friend was still in terrible danger. There was also the matter of the murder I had witnessed and the fate of James of the Glens, who I knew was innocent of the crime, but was languishing in prison. In the morning I went for a walk with Rankeillor and asked for his advice.

"You must do everything you can to help Mr. Thomson," he told me. "He has risked his life for you and it's right you do the same. The other matter is less clear. It is my opinion that you were only a witness to the incident, and not a participant. I would not interfere."

"But my evidence could free an innocent man," I protested.

"If you surrender yourself as a witness, it is likely you will be hung as an accomplice."

"It is my duty to go," I replied.

"Well said," he cried. "You must do what you think is right. There are worse things that can happen to you in life than to be hung. And if you think I am a fool for saying that, consider your uncle. And now," he continued, taking a letter from his cloak, "give this note to my bank in Edinburgh. They will give you the credit you need to help your friend with his travel arrangements."

Mr. Rankeillor smiled, shook my hand and wished me luck.

We set out for Edinburgh, Alan and I, walking slowly and finding it hard to share our thoughts. The time of our parting was approaching, and I felt sad at the loss of my friend, after all our adventures together.

We made our plans. Alan would hide in the open country, coming once a day to some woods where I could leave him messages. There was an Appin lawyer

he had heard of in Edinburgh, who might be trusted to secure a ship bound for France. I promised I would find him.

At last, we were standing on the brow of a hill, looking out over the city and the sea. We both knew it was time to separate.

"Goodbye to you," whispered Alan, holding out his hand.

"Goodbye" I answered, and gave his hand a squeeze. Then I set off down the hill.

We didn't look each other in the face, and I didn't turn around to catch a last glimpse of him as I walked away. But I felt so lost and lonely, I wanted to sit down by the side of the road and weep like a baby.

At noon I entered the city. I'd never visited one before and was stunned by the huge height of the buildings, some stretching up to fifteen floors or more; the narrow streets that spewed out pedestrians like a stream bursting through a set of rapids; the sparkling goods on display in a hundred shop windows; the hubbub and noise; the foul smells and fine clothes everywhere. I let the crowd carry me along, gazing at the sights. But all the time there was a cold gnawing in my stomach, a sense of something missing. I thought of my friend, alone and hiding in the heather. I thought of all our adventures and realized that, without Alan by my side, they would soon be no more than memories. In time these would fade, until they felt like the scenes from a dream.

While I was wondering about my past, the rushing tide of the crowd carried me to the steps of Mr. Rankeillor's bank, and on to my next adventure.

About Robert
Louis Stevenson

When the end came it surprised nobody. From the age of three, Stevenson had experienced severe problems with his breathing and his lungs. Every few months he would have an attack of breathlessness and bleeding. On several occasions his doctors had told him he had only weeks left to live. Although he was never diagnosed as suffering from tuberculosis, his symptoms match those of the disease. His quest for a dry and healthy climate to improve his condition had taken him as far from his homeland as he could get, to the Pacific islands of Samoa. Here his family hoped that his lungs were at last growing stronger. But a few weeks after his forty-fourth birthday, in 1894, he had a stroke and died within minutes. He was buried in a tomb on the mountain that overlooked his home.

It had been an eventful life, and the last chapter of it was perhaps the most extraordinary. For six years prior to his death he roamed the Pacific Ocean, hopping from island to island in small trading boats or chartered yachts, visiting the scattered communities of the South Seas.

Perhaps he was always destined to take to the sea. His father's family were engineers and had designed and constructed most of the lighthouses around the treacherous Scottish coastline. Louis, as he was called by his friends, was a gifted but sickly child. He studied engineering, thinking he might go into the family business, but he changed his mind and switched his studies to law, receiving his degree in 1875. However, as a student he had been busy submitting essays and short stories to magazines, and shortly after graduating he announced to his family that he wanted to be a writer.

All the major events of his life were punctuated by his poor health. While he was in France, in 1876, trying to recover from a bout of illness, he met the American Fanny Osbourne and fell in love. By now Stevenson was making his name as a travel writer. He used the incidents of his life – as he always would – as the material for his books. He pursued Fanny to America – documented in *Across the Plains* (1883) – and they were married. Even their honeymoon – at an old mining camp in the Californian wilderness – supplied him with a new book: *The Silverado Squatters* (1883).

But it was *Treasure Island* (published in book form in 1883) that made his name. Begun as a bedtime story to be told to his stepson, Lloyd, Stevenson at last proved to himself that he could write full-length novels. In the next five years he was prolific, penning his classics, *Kidnapped* and *The Strange Case of Dr.*

Jekyll and Mr. Hyde, as well as letters, plays, and short stories.

On June 26, 1878, Stevenson's greatest adventure began. He set sail from San Francisco with Fanny, Lloyd and his mother, thinking he would be away a year, voyaging around the South Seas. He was never to return to his beloved Scotland. As their ship, *The Casco*, sailed deep into the Pacific, Stevenson's health improved, and so did his writing.

His early travel books had been presented in the voice of a lively, flippant narrator. As he saw more of life in the Pacific Islands, he became a gritty social commentator – a reversal of his earlier ambitions in writing: always to entertain. He was directly involved in local political affairs, visiting a leprosy colony and defending the priest who ran it, and protesting against the German authorities in Samoa, where he eventually settled. His later stories – *The Beach at Falesa* (1893), for example – dealt with the corruption and exploitation of the islanders by European and American traders and missionaries.

The book he was working on when he died, *The Weir of Hermiston* (published unfinished in 1896) is regarded by many modern critics as his masterpiece. Despite the tremendous odds against him, Stevenson's hard work, stamina and, above all, his curiosity helped him to triumph in the end, and earn his place in the library of the classics.

Movies

There have been dozens of movie versions of *Kidnapped*, but none really stands out as definitive. Perhaps the best three are:

The 1971 production, with Michael Caine improbably cast as Alan Breck, and a creepy Donald Pleasence as Ebenezer. One critic described Caine's performance as a "wonderful mix of swagger and intelligence". Michael Caine had already starred in a comedy adaptation of another story by Stevenson, *The Wrong Box* (1966).

The 1959 Disney production starring Peter Finch as Alan and James MacArthur as David. The screenplay was written by a Disney director, Robert Stevenson, but despite the name, he's not related to Robert Louis Stevenson.

A 1978 mini-series with David McCallum as Alan Breck. In an interview about the series published in the UK's *TV Times*, Glasgow-born McCallum said, "I'm a lowland Scot playing a Highlander with a New York accent."

Many of the movie versions include some scenes from *Catriona*, a sequel to *Kidnapped* that Stevenson completed in 1893. It describes Davie's return to the Highlands and the trial of James of the Glens.